CHADRON (NE) STATE COLLEGE
3 5086 00374070 9

W9-BSO-521

Carolina Hurricane

By the Same Author

BEAVER OF WEEPING WATER

DANGER ON SHADOW MOUNTAIN

DEVIL'S DOORSTEP

HIGH COUNTRY ADVENTURE

LION ON THE RUN

LOST IN THE DESERT

THE SEAL OF FROG ISLAND

SHIPWRECK BAY

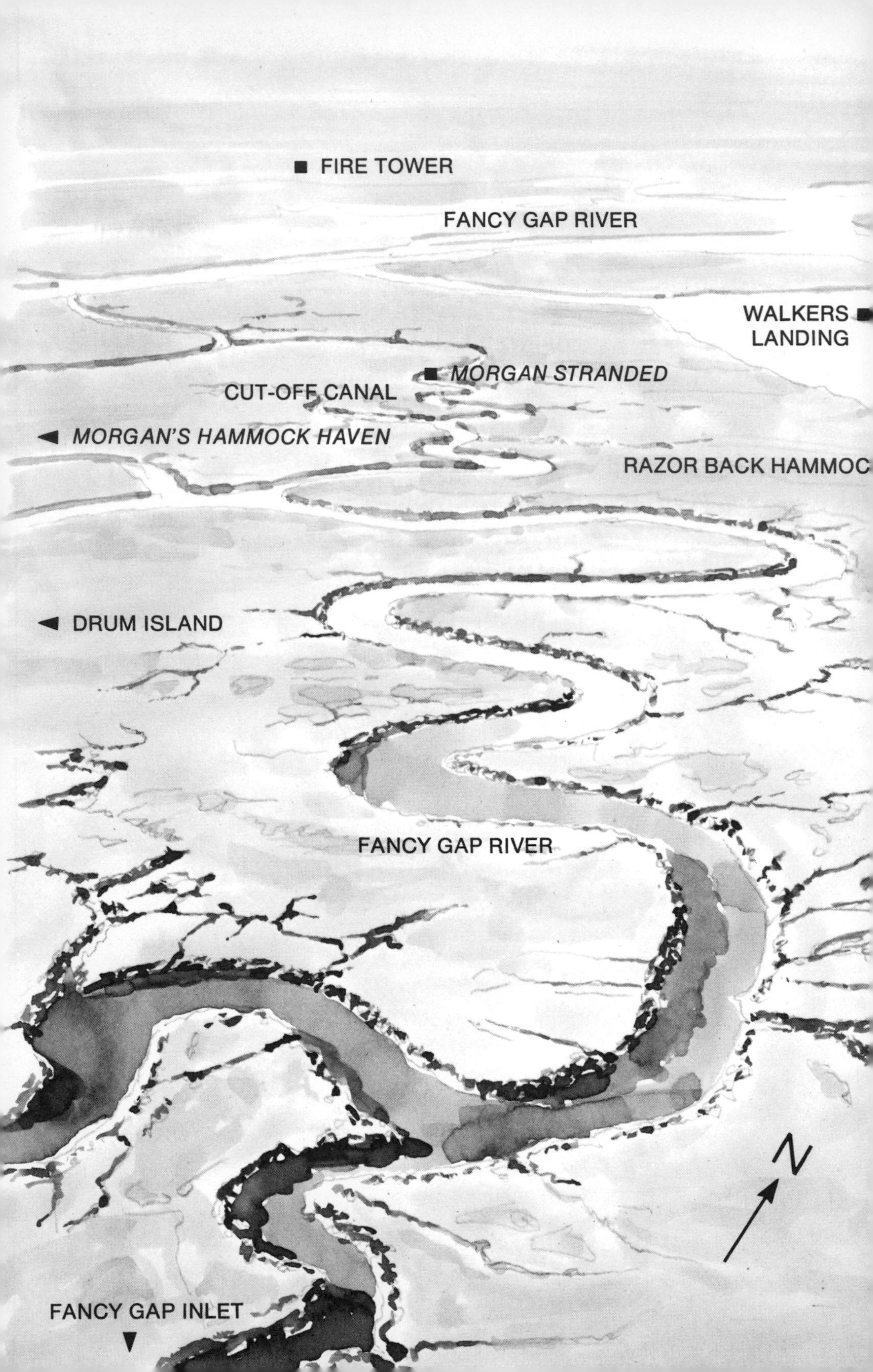
FIRE TOWER
FANCY GAP RIVER
WALKERS LANDING
MORGAN STRANDED
CUT-OFF CANAL
MORGAN'S HAMMOCK HAVEN
RAZOR BACK HAMMOC
DRUM ISLAND
FANCY GAP RIVER
N
FANCY GAP INLET

Carolina Hurricane

MARIAN RUMSEY

Illustrated by Ted Lewin

WILLIAM MORROW AND COMPANY
New York 1977

Printed in the United States of America.

1 2 3 4 5 6 7 8 9 10

Library of Congress Cataloging in Publication Data

Rumsey, Marian.
Carolina hurricane.

SUMMARY: Lost in a crab boat in the middle of a South Carolina salt marsh, twelve-year-old Morgan endures the full brunt of a hurricane. [1. Hurricanes—Fiction] I. Lewin, Ted. II. Title.
PZ7.R888Car [Fic] 77-5622
ISBN 0-688-22128-9
ISBN 0-688-32128-3 lib. bdg.

For Karen

Contents

Carolina Hurricane

1
A Problem with Tater

Painting the front porch was not Morgan's idea of a good way to spend his Saturday morning. He slid the paint bucket to one side and looked back at his progress. At least half of it was finished, but he still had the turned posts to do. That was going to take him forever. Inside the house the phone began to ring, and he wondered if it could be Freddy calling to see if he could come into town for the ball game. Morgan made a face. How had he ever been so dumb as to suggest painting the porch? Admittedly it had been his own idea. Father had been busy studying to pass his exam for his towboat pilot's license, and Morgan had felt he should help him out. He pulled the bucket farther forward as Mother opened the front door.

"What's wet?" she asked.

"Nothing down there yet. Who was on the phone? Was it Freddy?"

Mother walked down the steps, and for a moment she stood silently staring into the sky. Then she said, "No, it was Mr. Winslow at the cannery."

Morgan waved his brush excitedly. "Does he have our check made out for last week's catch?" Morgan always looked forward to receiving his share of the money.

"Yes, it's there, and I'll pick it up later." She turned around and looked the other way. "He was also concerned about the weather."

Morgan tugged the bucket up another few inches, then squinted at the world through the porch posts. "You mean here? Our weather?" He went down the steps to stand beside her in the grass. "What's up?"

Mother looked at the horizon thoughtfully. "That tropical depression offshore has suddenly built up to a full storm. It's predicted to pass us offshore, but a hurricane watch has been posted for our area. That means we must watch its movements very closely."

Morgan sucked in his breath. "A hurricane!"

Mother nodded. "Mr. Winslow knows Father is in Charleston taking his exam, and he thought we might not have been listening, which we haven't been. But the barometer has been quite high, and it's been so lovely the past few days that it seemed a little unnecessary."

Morgan looked across the yard and to their dock. Father's crab boat was tied up there along with a pile of traps he was going to repair when he came home. In any bad-weather front, Father always took in the pots in order to save his catch of crabs as well as to prevent the traps from being dragged in the high water and waves and lost. Morgan looked beyond the dock at the endless maze of islands that stretched before him as far as he could see. He had lived in the low-country tidelands of the South Carolina salt marsh for all of his twelve years, and it was as familiar a place to him as their yard in which he stood.

"I suppose Mr. Winslow thought we should take in the traps," he said finally.

"Yes, he believed it would be best. He said there is a low-pressure system building inland, and that's worrisome. You know how flighty a hurricane can be in the changing direction it takes."

"Nearly all of the storms miss us entirely," Morgan said carefully.

Mother nodded. "That's true, but we mustn't risk not preparing for the worst. Yet if I call Father, he's apt to drop everything and rush home, and it might not be necessary at all."

"If he did come, it would mean he wouldn't get his license!"

Mother pounded her fist on the porch rail. "Exactly!" She looked at Morgan. "I told Mr. Winslow I didn't want to bother Father in Charleston. I told him we knew what to do and would take care of everything and thanked him for calling."

Morgan relaxed. "At least that's settled." Yet he knew that the storm could change its course unexpectedly and come straight for them. "Well, it looks great right this minute," he said thoughtfully.

"Yes, doesn't it ever," Mother agreed. "It's nearly as nice as yesterday."

Morgan nodded and stared at the cloudless sky.

It was a pale, whitish blue, and he wondered if perhaps there weren't some very high clouds to give it that color. Yet the only inkling of any advancing weather, that he could see, might be the filmy halo around the sun. But the best of weather could precede the actual storm. And rain. They would doubtless get lots of rain. "I think I should start taking in the traps now while it's still nice out," he said.

Mother sighed. "Yes, that's the first thing; we definitely can't afford to lose any of them. At the moment, fishing blue crabs is our bread and butter." She started back up the steps; then she hesitated and looked at Morgan's half-completed work. "Why must everything happen at once? It would have been nice to get this painting finished. If I have time, I'll do it. But there are a million things I must attend to first."

"Father's tools have to be moved off the back porch," Morgan said. "If it rains, that roof leaks like a sieve."

Mother chewed at her lip. "And there's all the loose junk in the yard that must be put in the garage. Thank goodness the storm shutters are in good shape in case we need them. You'll have hard work pulling the pots and bringing them home."

"Oh, that's not work! You know I do it alone when Father works part time on the mill towboat. And I won't have to hurry; I can take my time. Since it's only a hurricane watch, I probably still have a few more hours of gorgeous weather. Besides I really would rather pull pots than anything!"

Mother cocked her head and laughed. "I know! For you, it's paradise compared to painting the porch!"

Morgan grinned, turned in a leap, and bolted for the garage. "Yippee!" Storm or not, his Saturday was going to turn out all right after all. He pulled open the double doors. "Come on, Tater!"

The big brown Labrador retriever that had been locked inside danced out with a rush, ran twice around him at full speed, and then dashed for the house.

"Keep him off the porch!" Mother shrieked. "The paint!"

"Tater! Come back!" Morgan shouted. He ran, caught the dog around the middle, and pulled him back down the steps. "Come on! We're going in the boat!"

Those were Tater's magic words. Suddenly he

began to bark furiously; he ran across the grass, over the wooden plank gangway, and down their dock. It was a long jump into the boat tied there, but Tater made it in one easy leap. Then he scampered from thwart to thwart, bow to stern, and back again, rattling the oars and barrels and tangling himself in the lines and buoys.

"Silly mutt," Morgan said affectionately, as he found the extra gas can in the garage and carried it down to the pier. Next he jumped into the boat and methodically began to toss everything in it out onto the dock.

Suddenly there was a splash behind him. Morgan looked up. Tater had leaped over the rail and into the water. Quickly he swam once around the boat, came back, put one large, webbed paw and his nose on the gunwale, and looked inside with a wet, happy face. "No, you can't get back in; I'm busy," Morgan told him, as he threw a crab pot to the dock. Instantly the dog turned, swimming in and out through the pilings of the pier and up to their shell beach. He climbed out of the water and spotted Mother coming across the grass. Tater bolted straight for her, skidded to a stop, and shook himself thoroughly.

Mother gasped. But Tater was off again at a run. He bounded down the dock and jumped back into the skiff beside Morgan, getting him wet and setting the boat to rocking as if it were in a heavy sea.

"Honestly," Mother complained, as she brushed at her wet slacks, "lock up that animal for five minutes, and he acts like a fizzing bomb. Here. I packed you a lunch; it's almost that time, and I know you'll be hungry."

Morgan peeked into the picnic basket she had put down on the dock. "Chocolate cake!" Now he was more anxious than ever to be off. He turned on the fuel, pulled out the choke, and started up the eighteen-horsepower motor on the first attempt. For a moment he was enveloped in the whitish smoke bubbling from the exhaust and the familiar smell of oily gasoline.

"You take care now," Mother told him, "and I'll expect you back home by suppertime. You're probably right about this beautiful weather lasting a while longer. You should have plenty of time to take in the traps and get on home before the rain begins."

"Sure enough," Morgan answered. He put the engine into gear and idled into the channel. Tater was in the bow. He stood with his feet on the very stem and looked alertly ahead as if he were the captain of his own ship. Morgan knew the dog was completely content. Tater loved boat rides nearly as much as swimming.

"See you later!" he shouted to Mother on the dock. She smiled, waved, and then Tater barked twice. That was Morgan's signal. He throttled up, and the boat picked up speed.

The tide was with him, so Morgan was able to make good time. As he covered the miles down Fancy Gap River, he was as satisfied with his life as Tater, for he loved every inch of their twenty-foot crab boat. It had been one of the best days of his life when, a year ago, Father had told him that he considered Morgan old enough to handle the boat alone. And then, six months later, Father had asked him if he would like to work the pots alone when he went out on the towboat. Morgan had nearly fainted with happiness, for to him, working the crab-pot sets wasn't work at all. Each time he pulled one of the familiar wire traps there was always a thrill of anticipation as he wondered how many big blue crabs he would find. And Father always made certain that he received his fair share of the profits. Morgan was the only boy he knew who held such an enviable position and had a nice bank account besides.

He pulled the picnic basket closer to the control panel, and with one hand he rooted about for what he wanted. Dessert first! He bit into Mother's delicious cake, devouring every morsel with enthusiasm and licking each finger with a terrible show of manners. With his other hand he steered. The tidal river was narrow and winding as it made its way to the sea, and the boat skimmed along almost as if it knew its way alone. As each bend appeared Morgan guided it with such ease that the boat banked gently around the curve and always perfectly in midstream. Now and again he touched the wheel a tiny bit more than usual; the boat turned ever so slightly and missed a batch of floating marsh grass. But always, with as light a touch, Morgan turned the wheel back again as he headed straight down the channel at top speed. Occasionally he glanced astern. As he did, Morgan could see his wake, which cut the dark-green water like a pair of silver wings.

Continually he came upon feeding common egrets and the great blue herons walking along in the mud or wading knee-deep along the shores. Some would stop in midstep, turn, and point their long bills toward him with calm indifference. Others, more nervous, would bend their knees and seem to jump into flight. With the appearance of flying in slow motion, they would rise majestically up and over the hump of marsh grass and slowly flap away. Often above the noise of the engine, Morgan heard the shrill *scree-scree* of blackbirds as they jittered about in the grasses. Once he spotted the blue, black, and white colors of a kingfisher that was sitting vigilantly on a piece of flotsam. Another time he saw an osprey circling high overhead.

But Morgan's favorite marsh birds were the flocks of tiny sandpipers. They gathered like brown clouds and ran like the wind along the sticky mud or the occasional stretch of shell beach. Then, seemingly without warning and as one tightly knit unit, they would abruptly change their direction and scurry a different way. Just as suddenly, without a single bird's hesitation and with a flash of white underbodies, the little flock would take to the air. Soon they would quickly descend, and as they glided to a landing their tightly knotted group would once more dash off down the beach with a blur of their dainty matchlike legs.

It hardly seemed any time at all to Morgan before he began to spot the red-and-white buoys that marked his crab sets. Yet he passed the floats, one by one, until finally the river widened. Then the marsh disappeared on the one side and was replaced by the shining, white sand of a low spit of land that separated him from the sea.

Morgan slowed the boat, and he began to scan the water. It was time now for him to start pulling his crab pots. He would bring them in and slowly work his way back toward home. He spotted his first float. Instantly he idled the boat toward it and picked up the short-handled hook beside the wheel. As he came alongside the buoy, he snagged it with the metal clip and pulled it into the boat, while at the same time he turned the wheel and put the boat into a very tight circle. Seconds later he had the float's attached mooring line over the roller chock on the rail, and with its help he easily pulled it in hand over hand. Within moments, the wire crab pot appeared on the surface; he leaned over the rail again, lifted the trap into the boat, and admired his first catch.

They were six mean-looking customers with snapping claws, and Morgan was pleased to see that only one of the blue crabs was legally undersized. He pulled on his heavy rubber work gloves, flicked open the trap's top, and plucked out the youngster. He slammed the lid and relatched it. Then he held up the crab and faced him eye to eye.

"Now listen carefully," he instructed. "You go straight home and eat heartily. I'll catch you again in a few more months."

He threw the crab back into the water, and it swam hastily into the depths. So much for acting silly. He turned to the wheel, but before he could put the boat on course, there was a gigantic splash. Morgan knew instantly that it was Tater, jumping in for another swim. He waited patiently until the dog finally came to him, put his paw on the rail, then his nose, and woofed throatily. Morgan grinned, wrapped his arms around the animal's shoulders, and then heaved him bodily inside the boat. Tater bobbed up and down with excitement, shook himself furiously, and stuck his wet nose into Morgan's hand.

"You are a drippy mess," he told the dog, as he went back to the wheel, turned it, and headed the boat for his next red-and-white float. Tater jostled past his legs and began to investigate the captives clicking in their cage.

"Watch your nose," he told the dog absently, as he idled the engine again, leaned over the rail, plucked out the buoy, pulled in the pot, and brought in his next catch. Right away Morgan knew that particular trap hadn't done well; he could tell by its weight. Once it had surfaced, he saw that it held only a small star drum. He opened the top, removed the fish, and tossed it into the bait barrel. Tater bounded up, stood on his back legs to look inside, and barked rapturously at the flapping finny. Morgan stacked the trap on top of the first, and in the same way stretched its mooring line neatly over the thwart. Back again to the wheel, and he started off. Tater bustled up to the bow and quivered in anticipation as they approached the next float.

For over three hours Morgan and Tater enjoyed their game of what-have-we-caught! At the end of that time, Morgan had brought in over sixty traps and had stacked them neatly in tiers, one atop the other, until now his boat resembled a wire sky-scraper afloat. There was a constant creeping motion about it as the crabs moved and climbed about inside their particular cages, and there was the all-permeating odor of undersea things, long-dead fish, and salt.

Now and then Morgan thought of Mother at home, moving everything that might blow away into the garage or else painting the porch, and he heaved a great sigh of relief that he wasn't there. It was far too grand a day to be stuck at home working. He brushed the back of his arm over his forehead. But it surely was hot! He rooted around in the small cuddy under the foredeck and found his straw hat. As he jammed it on his head he took time out for a moment to look around him.

Morgan had been steadily working his way back up the river, and he had been intent only on moving from crab pot to crab pot. Now he turned and looked behind him. What he saw made him gasp.

From where he was at that second, he had a full view of the entrance to Fancy Gap Inlet, that very spot where he had begun to pull his pots. But now it did not even slightly resemble the same place.

Huge breakers rolled into the inlet from the sea and rumbled through the entrance. White water, like foaming suds, gushed into the narrow waterway. Morgan could hardly believe his eyes. Luckily he and Father never set their crab pots in the ocean! If he had run that calm inlet three hours ago, he would never have been able to get back in again. It had become dangerous beyond words.

Morgan ran his tongue over his lips; he felt a prickling of uneasiness. Except for those immense, breaking seas gushing into the entrance, the water in the river was as glassy smooth and brilliant as a mirrored plate. There wasn't a breath of air. He stared mesmerized at the huge surf that pounded through that windless channel and at the mists that had risen over the beach. The Atlantic Ocean suddenly had become a seething, moving mass of rolling and thundering seas.

He climbed up and stood on the seat as he tried to see over the top of the marsh grass. It was difficult because the tide had changed, and it was ebbing. During the past hour his boat might as well have been slowly dropping into a canyon of mud that was topped with a fringe of green. Yet Morgan was able to see a heavy line of overcast sky on the horizon, and radiating out of the center of that line were thin streamers of high, white clouds. He stared fixedly at that point for a long while. For some reason that sky bothered him as much as those breaking seas at the inlet. For the first time all afternoon, Morgan again became thoroughly aware of the potential danger of the hurricane hovering offshore.

Tater came to him and stood at his side quietly; the dog's muzzle was raised toward the sea and clouds, and he was silently at attention. At that moment Tater seemed to have lost all of his silliness and become the mature, adult dog that he truly was. Morgan shot another troubled look at the horizon. The clouds were definitely moving toward him steadily and ominously. He turned to the heavy haze rising higher and higher over the surf that pounded at the inlet. Because they were being pushed ahead of the storm, those tremendous seas had taken only a few hours to build up. Morgan shook himself slightly. It was time to finish pulling the rest of his traps; it was time to be getting home.

Quickly he steered full speed for his next buoy. He had no more interest in his catch; now he was anxious to head back. Tater suddenly returned to his usual frisky and exuberant self, and he clattered up to the bow and began to bark excitedly. Morgan worked hard and fast, and the perspiration rolled off him in glistening drops. If only there was the barest stirring of air, the heat might not be so unbearable. Yet if there was any breeze, it never reached him in the tidal waterway.

Finally the last trap was in, and for a moment Morgan flopped down on the seat to rest. "It's never been so hot!" he panted to Tater. "It must be because of the storm."

The dog squirmed up to him happily; his tongue was hanging out. Tater was feeling the heat too.

But why wasn't there any wind? Morgan chewed at his lip tensely. It seemed eerily strange a hurricane could be offshore that moment and yet there wasn't a stirring of air. He looked across the opposite rail and stared restlessly at the clouded sky to the southeast. The overcast had come closer since the last time he had checked its progress. He gripped the gunwale of the boat fiercely. It was so still and quiet. The familiar marsh seemed to have become strangely unreal. Morgan brushed his hand over his forehead. It must be due to the heat; it was so stiflingly hot he felt as if he could hardly breathe. He gritted his teeth and asked himself what exactly did he know about a hurricane?

He had to admit he had no firsthand knowledge. Whenever one looked as if it would come anywhere near their town of Suggs Mill, Father rushed the whole family off to Varnville, fifty-four miles away, to stay with Grandmother Brian. And that far inland a hurricane was entirely different from one along the low country's marshy ocean shores. Except for flooding on the neighboring Coosawhachie and Salkehatchie Rivers, an offshore hurricane produced only a super-sized rainstorm in Varnville.

Yet even now Morgan recalled, when he had been very young, seeing what the world was like after a hurricane had passed their town. The family had returned home, one beautiful August day, after staying in safety with Grandmother Brian during the storm. Morgan could still remember the sight of their house as they drove up to it in the car. It was barely standing, nothing more than a rickety, roofless shell. Everything in it and around it had been destroyed by the violent, rampaging winds of the storm. Though at the time Morgan had been more concerned about his missing toys, he had known, in his very young way, that his family had lost everything they owned. But Father immediately began to rebuild the house; he built new traps, bought new boats, and they started all over again.

Since that time no other hurricane so destructive had ever come anywhere near their part of South Carolina. There had been times when they had been afraid one might. There had been times they had worked long and hard to prepare their house for that terrible threat. There were times they had listened to the hurricane watch turn into a hurricane warning, and Father had told them it was time to leave and go inland. Morgan had been older then; he had been frightened at the way Father and Mother listened tensely to the weather reports coming in on their radio. But always, at the last minute, the storms had turned away. Either they had gone far out to sea away from land, or they had speeded past and up the warm Gulf Stream and on north.

Morgan trembled with uneasiness. What if this hurricane changed its direction? What if the storm now offshore hit them after all? That would mean Mother and he would have to close up the house and go inland. Yet before they could leave, there would be a lot of hard work to do, and all of it without assistance from Father. They would have to put all the furniture upstairs to protect it from flooding and close the storm shutters. They would have to board up the garage and the front and back porches that would be filled with everything moveable from the yard. They would only have time to take the special things with them that they could carry in the car. They would have to get the heavy crab boat on its trailer and tow it behind the Buick. It would be packed to the very gunwales with clothes from the closets and the linen from the cupboard and all of Father's tools, everything the family would need to start all over again. Then they would call old Tater and drive away, leaving most of their life behind them. It hurt Morgan even to think about it.

Suddenly Morgan pushed the dog aside and stood up. "Let's shove off for home," he told Tater quickly. The afternoon was getting on; he wanted to reach the house by suppertime so Mother would not begin to worry. He definitely did not like the feel of the weather!

He shot another fidgety glance at the sky. The scud clouds were coming fast; he hated that darkening horizon. It looked as if the storm was heading straight for him! Then he took a long, steadying

breath. Even if it passed miles away from him, he knew that a hurricane always spread out a blanket of clouds ahead of its center; he knew there were bound to be overcast skies and squalls. Yet at the rate the overcast was moving in, it looked as if it would rain very soon. There was no need to get any wetter than necessary. At that moment he decided to take the Cut-Off Canal; the shortcut should save him over an hour in getting home.

As he started out, Morgan wished the tide wasn't against him; he wished he could get more speed out of his heavily loaded boat. And then he sucked in his breath sharply. Here came the breeze!

The silver-glazed water ahead of him suddenly shattered with dark blotches as cat's paws rippled over the surface toward him. As the wind touched the boat, it was stronger than he expected. It was a sudden, small gust. And it was not at all refreshing. It was like a fan blowing across a hot stove.

"The start of the storm," Morgan said through his clenched teeth. He saw the wind was coming out of the northeast, which put the hurricane's center about opposite him, where it was supposed to be. Another fitful, hot gust wafted over him; the spartina grass high on the tidal banks fluttered lightly. Morgan's dark eyebrows nearly met over his nose as he frowned fiercely. A flock of egrets had risen high into the sky and flown off to the west. It looked as if they had taken off at the first breath of that sticky wind. There were also large blue herons and the little blue herons in the air, and then more egrets appeared. A scattering of gulls shrieked past overhead.

Morgan jerked his eyes back to the waterway. The shortcut canal to town was right ahead. He had to take it slowly as he came up, for the tide was running out fast, and the entrance bar was shallow.

Yes, he could see the turn. Morgan idled the engine, and the boat began to lose way. Then he sucked in his breath in dismay. The mud extended from each shore at the small entrance; it nearly blocked off the canal entirely from the wider and deeper river. He stared at the narrow channel he had planned to take in order to save precious time. Then he looked at the sky. Clouds were directly overhead, and behind them was a layer that was thicker yet. Another sudden, hot flutter of wind riffled the water.

"It would have to be the full of the moon," Morgan said, suddenly realizing why the tides were lower than usual.

He ran his tongue over his parched lips. His boat drew a foot and a half of water, and he could still run the motor if he had two feet. He shook his head; he doubted if there was that much water at the canal entrance. If he could only get over the bar! The canal had always been deep enough for the boat, but he knew he better not risk it. He would have to take the long way back to town. He would get home far later than he planned, and Mother would be upset about his not arriving on time, but it was better to be late than to get stuck on the bar. And, with luck, he still should make it home before dark.

Another light gust of wind hit him, and as it did Tater suddenly jumped off his favorite seat in the bow. He ran aft looking over the rail, sharply at attention. Not more than twenty feet away from him, and standing in the mud, were a pair of blue herons. They had probably begun to fidget when the breeze touched them, and the dog had become aware of their presence. Morgan realized instantly what was about to happen.

"Tater! No!" He lunged for the dog, missed him, and crashed headlong into the bait barrel. By then Tater was already into the water and had begun to swim to the bank. He had every intention of giving chase to those two birds. Yet Morgan

knew he hadn't a chance in the world of ever catching them, for the second Tater had splashed over the side, the birds had flown away. Nevertheless, Tater swam on to shore, lumbered out onto the mud with enthusiasm, barked loudly, then galloped up the bank, into the marsh grass, and disappeared.

Morgan moaned. "Tater! Come back!" He turned the boat; he would have to beach it on the mud! He kicked a crab-pot buoy aside with a crash, found the bowline, and, once the boat bumped aground, leaped ashore. Morgan sank into mud to his knees. Muttering under his breath, he rushed up the bank to the top of the marsh.

"Tater!" he screamed.

But then he skidded to a stop in the high grass and let out his breath in a groan. The dog was a running, leaping, brown missile. He was dashing full speed on across the marsh far, far ahead of him. As he ran, he scattered birds into flight to his right and left. He was barking, howling, yipping; he was having the time of his life. Tater loved to chase any kind of bird for the fun of it.

"Tater, there are times when I believe you would make good bait in one of my crab traps!" Morgan growled, as he hastily tied up the boat.

There was no doubt about what he had to do. He had to go after Tater and drag him back. The dog was dumb and foolish and silly, but Morgan loved him. He certainly would never leave him out on the marsh alone with a storm offshore.

2
Stranded

Morgan spun on his heels and began running across the marsh. But he knew the moment he started that to chase after Tater was probably useless. Tater usually had to run himself to near exhaustion, and only then would he come back. But Morgan ran after him all the same. He called; he shouted; he begged; he screamed. His efforts were a waste of time. Tater continued in his own determined and ridiculous way exactly as he pleased.

Finally Morgan came to a breathless halt. He had followed the dog for nearly a quarter of a mile, and now he had reached the end of the marsh island. Before him was a narrow span of water of the Cut-Off Canal, and just galloping up the muddy bank of the island opposite him was Tater. He had swum to the opposite side only minutes before.

"Tater!" Morgan shouted angrily. "Come back here! We're going in the boat!"

But either Tater didn't care, or he didn't hear. He bolted off like a flash and frightened a flock of plovers into a shrieking takeoff. He was after them instantly, howling at the top of his lungs. Morgan sucked in his breath raggedly. There was no possible way to go after him unless he swam across the creek himself.

"You dopey dog," Morgan said, still breathless. He had no desire to go swimming now, nor would it do much good if he did. He would never be able to catch him; Tater was supercharged with energy. He looked exactly like a brown, bouncing ball as he bounded through the grass, along the opposite bank of the Cut-Off Canal. Morgan chewed at his lip thoughtfully. If he could get the boat over the entrance bar and bring it up this way, he could follow Tater. He had planned to go this way in the first place; it was the short cut home. Tater would be able to hear the outboard motor, and eventually he would come to him.

Morgan turned his face into the hot, sticky breeze. It was beginning to rain; a light mist was unmistakably falling. Glancing at his watch, he saw it was six o'clock. He ran back to the boat. If he wanted to get it over the bar into the canal, he had to hurry. The tide was falling every second.

And as if to prove him out, when he returned to the skiff, the water had dropped sufficiently so that the boat was grounded firmly on the mud. It was a difficult struggle to push it into deeper water. By the time he had it floating, he was thoroughly wet and muddy.

But there was no time to waste! Quickly he tilted up the motor and flicked the lock lever down. He snatched up the bowline and started to tow the boat over the mudbank. But halfway across the bar, the boat slowed, grounded, and stopped. No amount of pulling moved it any farther. Morgan splashed to the stern, gripped it firmly, and pushed violently. Soft mud oozed around his feet. It felt horrible, but there was no time to worry about his comfort. At last the boat moved ahead!

But it didn't move far. The skiff bumped to a halt and stuck fast. Morgan readjusted his feet. Putting all of his strength into it, he pushed again. The boat squirmed ahead a tiny bit more; then it slid to another firm stop.

Rushing to the bow, Morgan swung the bowline over his shoulder, leaned into it, and pulled fiercely. His teeth clenched, eyes closed, and perspiration dribbling down his cheek, he could not remember when he had worked harder.

Suddenly, like a pea popping out of its pod, the boat shot forward. He had finally forced it into the deeper water of the canal. But as it floated free, the forward momentum shoved it straight into his back and sent him reeling face down in the water. When he surfaced, Morgan was gasping and sputtering, yet infinitely pleased. He was ready to go!

But first he climbed the bank to the top of the marsh for one more look for Tater. He frowned. Now the world had become shrouded in veils of mists. He could hardly see a hundred yards in any direction.

"Tater!" he called. But there neither was sight

of the dog nor was there sound of him. He faced into the wind. It was warm and wet, and it blew in fitful gusts. And now the sun nearly had disappeared. It was only a yellowish-white blur, and even as he watched it dimmed almost completely. Above the mists were heavier, thicker clouds. Morgan ran back down the bank. He had to move the boat up the canal to where he had last seen Tater.

It was nearly impossible. The boat had to be in deep water before he started the outboard, but now the tide and the increasing wind constantly forced the heavily loaded boat toward the narrow canal's shallow bank. He set the oars in the oarlocks and maneuvered back and forth continually as he tried to stay in deeper water. At last he was able to start the engine. He was off!

He reached forward into the cuddy and brought out his small, portable VHF weather radio. It was misting more heavily than ever now, and he was forced to wrap a rain slicker around the set to protect it from the moisture. But nothing had changed. The hurricane, now named Hetty, still fumed along with ninety-two miles an hour of wind in its center, and it was positioned to his east. Morgan listened tensely to the instructions being given for the hurricane watch in his area. He thought miserably of Mother. She would be sick with worry about him, for he was long overdue at the house. She would probably call Father, and he would rush to the airport and fly straight home to begin a search for him. Everything was going wrong!

He clicked off the radio. At least the hurricane was still heading away from him and was not gaining strength. And it was moving very fast. At the rate it was going, it would be gone before he knew it. Yet this didn't bring Morgan any great sense of relief. The visibility was still terrible, the mist was really a drizzle, and worst of all the wind was picking up strength moment by moment.

Morgan squinted into the gloom. That looked like the place coming up where he had last seen Tater. Yes, there were his footprints in the mud. Morgan frowned. Although he hated to leave the boat beached, he had to stop and climb the bank again to look for the dog. He might be gone for a while, and he didn't want to risk having the boat stranded permanently by the falling tide. There was only one thing to do. He turned off the engine and tossed out the anchor. He would have to wade ashore.

Morgan sat on the rail, dangled his toes in the warm water, and then hopped out. His feet touched bottom almost instantly, but to his horror they didn't stop! He sank into mud far past his knees.

"Oh!" he gasped, startled. His feet felt as if they had become cemented in sticky glue. He couldn't move! His ankles might as well have been bound tightly together. He grabbed at the boat beside him, but the wind had swung it out of reach, and he plunged forward. Surprisingly, lying in the water made it easier to force his legs into movement. He thrashed furiously, and he dragged one foot out of the sucking mud. He kicked again and managed to free his other leg. Then, like a snake, he slithered along the surface and finally reached firmer footing. He struggled to his feet and lunged forward, only to stumble over a piece of submerged driftwood and fall heavily to his knees. Mud splashed into his face; it was black, slimy, and smelled bad. He dragged himself to his feet unsteadily, waded out of the water, and started up the bank. But it was so steep in that spot that he slipped in the slick mud and rolled back to the water's edge. For a moment he lay in the disgusting ooze. Then he pulled himself to his feet again, gritted his teeth, and charged as fast as he could straight at the bank. The surge of speed and a tight grip on the spartina finally sent him scrambling over the top.

Everywhere he looked the marsh grass moved in the wind in undulating green and silver waves. The sky, drizzling with rain, was dark with thick, low clouds, and it restricted his visibility almost completely. Tater was nowhere within his limited range of sight. He turned back to the canal and looked at the boat. It was headed into the current; it was safe enough at least to leave temporarily while he searched for the dog.

Morgan turned away from the water and began to shout. "Tater! Hey, Tater!" He cupped his hands around his mouth and faced into the wind. "Tater! Come here!" He turned to face another direction. "Tater, please, it's time to go in the boat!"

Nothing. There was only the wind and the dripping, drizzling mists. The world was dismal and gloomy and unfriendly. "Tater, please, come back!" he shouted. But there was no answering bark.

In his search, Morgan wandered back and forth across the island on which he had last seen Tater.

Occasionally he startled a small bird into flight, but never the egrets or herons. Obviously Tater had chased the larger birds to one of the other islands. Once, as he stopped to call the dog, Morgan heard a low, distant rumble, and he knew at once that it was thunder. He began to hurry; he shouted for Tater more loudly and more often. The salt marsh was no place to be caught in a thunderstorm.

Eventually he crisscrossed the entire island, and once more he was faced with the canal. He stared at it miserably. Had Tater swum to still another island? "Oh, Tater, wherever are you?" he whispered.

He looked down the steep bank at the canal below him. He frowned. Far behind him was his anchored crab boat. It was sitting in a thin strip of water at the bottom of a muddy tidal hole. Quickly Morgan slid down the bank and began to run along the beach. Since he had left the boat, the tide had dropped so much that now he had only a few muddy steps before he could climb over the rail. There was no reason to stay anchored any longer; he might as well take the boat farther up the canal and search another island.

He pulled up the anchor and started up the

channel. Ahead of him was a gloomy sight. There was rain and wind and increasingly shadowy clouds. And mud! Nearly everywhere there was mud. Never had he seen the tide so low. He knew it must be due to the minus tides combined with the increasing northeast wind, which came from an inland direction along this stretch of easterly running coast. Every drop of water seemed to be roaring straight out of the canal. Morgan knew he should try to get out of the canal and reach the deeper river. But that would mean leaving Tater behind, which he couldn't do!

Morgan shot a look overhead. Through the drizzle it was dark with ugly, fast-moving clouds, and beyond him lightning flickered. The thundershower was heading directly for him. Then, as he rounded another bend, a sudden, intense gust of wind swept down the channel and sent his hat sailing off his head. He snatched for it, missed, and turned momentarily to watch it tumble like a spinning wheel into the bank.

Without warning, he lurched forward and hit the control panel; the boat had rammed the bottom violently. There was a heavy, grinding sound as the propeller plowed into mud. The motor slowed, sputtered, and nearly stopped, Morgan sucked in his breath, whirled the wheel, and veered to the right. Instantly the boat settled back into deeper water, and the motor picked up speed again.

Morgan breathed. The canal only had sufficient depth for his boat in the very center of the narrow channel! He realized he would have to pay very careful attention to steering. A second later the boat bumped again; the motor coughed and faltered as the propeller churned into another mound of mud.

Right away Morgan realized he was in serious trouble. He knew, without any doubt, that he was directly in midchannel. He ran his tongue over his lips. What was happening? Where had all the water gone? Quickly he began to rock the boat back and forth by shifting his weight from side to side. At once the motor picked up speed and ran more easily; he had surged forward into deeper water.

Suddenly a bolt of lightning flashed in jittering, jagged daggers in front of him, and Morgan flinched violently. He began to count, "A thousand one, a thousand two, a thousand three, a thousand—"

Thunder crashed over the noise of the engine.

The shower front was less than a mile away from him; already the drizzle was getting heavier. The wind suddenly gusted sharply and pushed him ever so slightly off course.

Again the boat hit bottom; he heard the propeller throbbing through mud. It was difficult to steer well when he traveled so very slowly; he barely had control of the boat.

Another brilliant streak of lightning lit the world and momentarily blinded him. Morgan nearly danced with nervous impatience. It was almost impossible to see exactly where the banks were located in the drizzling rain or to tell which way he should turn to reach deeper water. Thunder boomed deafeningly. Suddenly the motor caught as the boat lurched over the mud; once more it was under way.

Again lightning flashed in a blinding white streak; the ear-splitting crash of thunder seemed to rock the boat with its intensity. The wind gusted furiously, and sheets of rain pelted down in torrents. Morgan could see nothing at all. Suddenly the motor stopped without warning, and almost instantly the boat struck bottom with a grinding crash.

Everything seemed to happen then. The wind

screamed and whipped at him; the rain stung at his face and arms; the flash and roar nearly became unbearable. Morgan stumbled forward as he tried to reach the protection of the tiny, covered shelter in the bow. But he hadn't taken two steps when the boat rocked violently and a dark shape scrambled over the rail and landed in his arms. Morgan leaped backward, startled; he slipped and fell with a crash onto the floorboards with the great weight on top of him. In one second he realized what had happened.

"Tater!" he gasped. The dog wriggled like an eel as he tried to climb under the thwart beside him. He was squishing with wet hair and mud. Morgan shoved the dog aside and sat up, running his hand over his forehead to brush away the rain that poured into his eyes. Tater turned and crawled into his lap, pushing his head under Morgan's arm. Of course, he should have known all along what would bring Tater back to the boat! The dog loved the rain, but he hated lightning and thunder more than anything on earth. Morgan pressed his hands over Tater's ears and held him tightly. Surprisingly, giving comfort to Tater lessened Morgan's own nervousness.

It was a long time before the shower moved on and they finally confronted a quieter world that once more began to take on familiar shapes and forms. The rain slackened into a wind-whipped sprinkle, and the sky lightened infinitesimally. Tater moved, looked up, and wagged his tail. Morgan shook his head. To scold Tater for the trouble that he had caused was useless. So instead he smoothed the dog's dark, wet head and said thankfully, "I'm glad you came back." This time he tied the bowline of the boat to the dog's collar; he wasn't going to risk having Tater disappear again. Then Morgan stood up. He had work to do. Now that Tater had returned, he could start for home. What a relief that would be!

But before he could do anything, he faced the problem of getting the boat off the mud, for until then he could not possibly restart the engine. Morgan stared at the canal. At least he must get the boat back into what little water seemed to be left. The tide should have been nearly at a complete standstill, yet the water appeared to be rushing out of the canal as fast as ever. So many problems would be solved if the tide would change and the water come back into the marshlands. Not only would there be plenty of depth for the boat, the current would give him an added boost for the trip home. Morgan picked up an oar. He could not waste time waiting for the tide to turn.

He stumbled over Tater; the dog whined and pushed his nose into Morgan's hand. "Well, I'm sorry I stepped on you, but get out from under my feet." He patted the dog gently; then he began to pole the skiff to midstream. It wasn't easy. Constantly he fought the stiff wind that forced the towering trap-filled boat back against the bank. Then to his dismay, when he finally did reach center channel, he could tell by one jab of the oar straight down that he barely had enough water in which to run the outboard. He shoved Tater aside, tripped over the line attached to his collar, and finally managed to get the anchor overboard to hold the boat in place. He patted Tater again. "It won't be long now," he said cheerfully. "I'll get the motor going and head straight home." He went to the engine and pulled the starter cord.

He pulled it again, and then again, but it refused to start. Morgan checked the fuel tank, but it was still half full. He turned back to the engine and tripped over Tater huddled on his feet.

"Oh, will you please sit over there!" he said, moving the dog away from him. Again he tried to force the engine into life—time after time he pulled the starter cord—but it was no use. It had become as stubborn as a balky mule. Whatever was the matter with it? Then Morgan thought of the ugly, grinding noise he had heard. He wondered uneasily if he could have hit something besides soft mud and perhaps could have even broken the propeller.

He pushed Tater aside; the dog was forever under his feet. "Whatever's wrong?" Morgan asked with a frown. "The thunder's over, at least for the moment anyway, and it looks as if the sky might be lightening up the slightest bit." But, of course, Tater didn't understand. He put his nose into Morgan's hand, and he whined again. "Are you thirsty? There's a nice bucketful of fresh rainwater right here." He pushed the dog's nose to the pail, but Tater wasn't thirsty. Morgan sighed. "Well, I haven't time to hold you in my lap if that's what you want."

He turned back to the motor. It was important to find the problem and repair it immediately. He hurried to the stern and stared into the water, but it was dark and murky, and he couldn't see a thing. He tilted the motor forward on its bracket. Yet after inspecting the propeller blades, he was certain nothing was wrong with them. Then he caught his breath sharply and ran his tongue over his lips. Going slow and dragging the propeller on the bottom had clogged the water intake with mud. Possibly the motor had overheated badly! Quickly Morgan took the cover panel off the engine and kneeled on the floorboards to examine it carefully. Almost instantly he sat back and closed his eyes. He didn't have to be much of a mechanic to know what was wrong. The motor had a cracked head! It was ruined! Morgan stumbled back against the side of the boat, feeling overwhelmed. He had ruined his father's motor! Now Father would never trust him with the boat again. He should have been more careful; he knew well the danger of an overheated engine, but he had been so busy trying to keep the boat afloat that he had forgotten to check the cooling water.

Morgan stood for a moment with his hand on Tater's shoulder. He knew he couldn't repair the engine; it would have to be rebuilt at a shop. And without the engine, he would have to row home. It was a long way, and there was no time to waste; he had to start immediately. During the best of times rowing home would be a rugged trip, and now with the wind and tide against him it would be nearly impossible. The loaded boat was unbelievably heavy. He would have to lighten it before he ever could hope to make any time at all.

Morgan gritted his teeth. Obviously the heaviest thing in the boat was the engine. He swallowed. He couldn't possibly leave it behind! It was bad enough that he had ruined it, but at least it could be repaired. He would have to eliminate other heavy gear. With a sinking heart he realized he would have to leave the crab pots. Each one had a cement weight, and the piled-high traps gave the boat uncontrollable windage. As he tossed them onto the muddy canal bank, he knew there was a very good chance the pots might be lost forever. He tried not to think of what Father would say to him when they met next.

But at last he was ready to start; he had lightened the boat to the point where at least he could row it. Yet before he left, he ran to the top of the marsh. He had to take careful bearings to help find the crab traps when the weather settled down again.

Morgan stared out at the darkening marsh. The thundershower had cleared most of the heavy mists, and only sporadic raindrops splattered down on him from the overcast skies. But the hot, sticky wind was blowing steadily and stronger than ever. It whipped his hair into his face and flapped his wet clothes in sharp snaps. Far to the west he saw the tall fire tower at Suggs Mill.

"How I wish I was home," he said, with one last glance at the high land and the distant pines. Then he turned to face the sea and gasped in horror.

The heart of the hurricane, in all its savage ugliness, was there for him to see. The horizon seemed to have a great, mountainous grayish-black hump rising out of it, and in the last light of day, it was tinged with edges of blood red. Now and then jags of lightning blinked and went out as black squalls extended from its center in every direction. But Morgan could not wrench his eyes away from that central, vile, and forbidding mountain that appeared to have risen ominously out of the ocean. It was the most terrifying and menacing sight he had ever seen. He wrenched his eyes away from the frightening sight. With the three points of Razor Back Hammock, the fire tower, and Fancy Gap

Inlet lined up, he had a fix and knew exactly where he was leaving the traps.

Frantic to start for home, Morgan bolted down the bank. He had left Tater tied in the boat, and when the dog saw him coming, he strained at the line and whined. Quickly Morgan jerked the radio out from under the slicker and turned it on. Then he let out his breath in relief. The weather hadn't changed. The hurricane was still passing to the north of him. What he had seen just now was the bar of the storm, moving on by.

Morgan turned off the set, jammed it into the cuddy, then shoved the boat away from the bank. Settling himself on the thwart, he began to row furiously. He had to get out of the canal! The hurricane might be passing him by, but Morgan didn't trust it any more than he trusted a swamp rattler. And he didn't like the way the water was dropping. Even if the motor had been working, he couldn't have used it. There was not much more than a foot and a half of depth left in midchannel.

He knew the hurricane was affecting the water level. There was the combination of the minus tides, the dropping barometric pressure, and the increasing northeast wind. It must have been blowing at least twenty-five miles an hour right that minute; Morgan couldn't really tell its true strength down in this tidal gully. All the flats as far north as Walkers Landing drained out Fancy Gap Inlet. The more the wind blew from the northeast, the more the water would be forced out of the upper tidelands, although the tide was now supposed to have changed. In fact, Morgan was beginning to believe this whole part of the marsh might be completely drained. He'd better hurry.

Morgan shoved Tater aside with his elbow; the dog was trying to climb on the seat beside him. "Lie down somewhere, Tater," he said gently. "I'm having a hard enough time as it is." It was not easy to get much power into his strokes. If he dipped the blades as deeply as he should, the oars hit bottom and dredged mud. And always the current and the wind were against him. He was not making very good time.

It was hard work, and Morgan wasn't certain how long he rowed. Enough time had passed that it had grown almost totally dark; his hands were sore and his shoulders ached. Occasionally he had to stop and rest despite the fact that, when he did, he lost precious time. But soon he was back at work. It had become what seemed an endless chore of lean, dip, and pull.

Then it began to rain again; it wasn't a mist or a drizzle or a sprinkle, but a steady, heavy downpour. And at about the same time, he hit bottom. He was in midchannel and in the deepest water, but still the boat came to a complete halt. Another confused few minutes passed as he struggled back and forth, looking for a way to get over the mud. Tater restlessly jumped from thwart to thwart and whined. Finally Morgan went to the bow and began probing with the oar. It was only about eight inches deep.

Morgan groaned. He had at least a mile yet to go before he reached the deeper river. He and Tater would have to get out of the boat and lighten it. Distasteful as walking in the mud would be, at least then he could tow the boat. He had to reach the river! Even after he got there, he still had nearly eight more miles to town. He picked up a line and began to fashion a harness at one end to go over his shoulders. Suddenly Tater barked, and he looked up.

Morgan gasped. Not more than ten feet away from him was the bank, and hundreds of crabs were

walking up the muddy shoreline. Not the blues he caught in his traps, but the little fiddler crabs. Most of them had one oversized claw raised in the air, and they were marching purposefully ahead through the rain.

"Look at them! There are hundreds!"

But Tater had seen enough; he dropped back inside the boat. Quickly Morgan tied the dog's leash to his belt; then he stepped over the side and sank into soft mud over his knees.

"Come on, Tater. Hop on out. The crabs won't hurt you. I have to get the boat out of this canal!" He yanked the dog over the rail, and as Tater waded to the firmer beach he scattered the crabs momentarily. But then the crabs collected and continued on their way while Tater nervously tried to ignore them. Morgan pressed his lips into a tight, thin line. He knew it was nature's way. Somehow the fiddlers sensed there was going to be an extremely high tide after this very low one, and they were going inland to escape it.

Morgan hated the way his feet and legs sank into the mud; with each step he wondered if he might sink so deeply that he would never be able to pull himself out again. Then he felt the tug of the line holding the dog; at least Tater would never leave him.

"Please, tide, come back and fill the marsh with water," he said into the night.

But it didn't. The wind increased minute by minute, and the water continued to fall. The boat threatened to ground again and again, and each time it became more difficult to force the boat into motion. Morgan's world became encompassed by dense rain and the faint glow of his hands as they clutched the rope to his shoulder. Now he could not see the banks of the canal or even Tater, who was walking along the beach beside him. He struggled through the mud, continually using all of his strength to pull. Yet he never stopped; he kept remembering the sight of the storm center. It had frightened him and he wanted to get home.

Suddenly the boat was hard aground again; Morgan closed his eyes and pulled furiously. But this time nothing happened. Within minutes he collapsed against the side of the boat in exhaustion. It was impossible; he couldn't budge it an inch! He leaned over the boat's rail, picked up the lantern, and flicked the switch. He held up the light and peered into the canal ahead of him.

Sheets of rain and mud were all that he could see. There was no more water left at all. The center of the channel was only a trickle a few inches wide. Then Tater slopped up through the mud and stood beside him.

"We're stranded," Morgan said hoarsely.

3
Bad News

Morgan simply could not use the boat without water. He would have to sit right where he was and wait until the tide decided it was time to change.

"Are we ever going to get in late!" he said, staring at the mud ahead of him. For a moment he considered walking home. If the water was gone, he could leave the boat. Then he shook his head. It was true the canal was dry, but he knew Fancy Gap River wasn't. It was twenty feet deep! What would he do when he walked up and faced it? He knew, too, that when the hurricane moved to the north of him, the wind would switch to the southwest and push the water back into the flats. It was going to boil in with a mighty rush, and without a boat he would be doomed. There was no choice; he would have to wait where he was.

"Come on, we have work to do," he said, and gave Tater a tug. But the dog put both forepaws against his shirt and whined.

Morgan patted him. "I know, you're upset. So are the birds, the crabs, and anything else stuck out here."

Morgan picked up his clam shovel. It was dark as pitch and pouring rain, but even so he could tell the boat was resting on an uneven lump of mud and was tipped violently to one side. He set to work shoveling what seemed to be melting black jello, and at last he succeeded in propping the boat firmly upright. Then he waded back through the mud, pulling Tater with him. Next he searched under a thwart and found the canvas tarpaulin. He flapped it open and began to erect a makeshift, protective tent over the boat. Finally he climbed under it, pulled Tater inside, and they sat huddled uncomfortably on the floorboards.

But this position was nearly as depressing as being out in the night and the drenching rain. One oar held the canvas upright for headroom, and it leaned precariously with each gust of wind. Rain streamed off the sides of the material and into the boat by the bucketful. It ran in small rivers along the bilge and gurgled noisily down the scuppers. The lantern's dim, yellowish glow illuminated the boat in shadowy flickers. Everything was wet and thickly splattered with the sticky, black mud, while lines, buoys, legs and pinchers of long dead crabs were lying about messily. There was a soggy orange life jacket beneath his hand, and the anchor, coated in slime and tangled in yards of its own rode, was under his feet. Further sharing the space were a small can of gasoline, fish bait, and one very soaked dog. Morgan leaned back against the hull of the boat with his knees tucked under his chin. He was tired and wet and dirty and hungry; life nearly wasn't worth living. He closed his eyes and listened to the pounding of the rain on the canvas, the moaning of the wind, and the faint sound of Tater's wagging tail flopping against the floorboards.

Morgan met the dog's eyes. "I'm glad you're here," he said, and put his hand on Tater's wet head. To be alone right then would have been unthinkable. How much Morgan wished he was home! But the next moment, he realized that home was going to be awful too. Mother would have called Father, worried because he didn't come back, and when Morgan got home and told him about the ruined motor and leaving all the traps behind, his father would never let Morgan run the crab pots again.

Miserably he pulled out the radio and tuned in to the weather. But Hetty hadn't changed; the hurricane was still offshore and moving quickly away from him.

Morgan was forced to sit idle beside Tater. There was nothing to do but listen to the driving rain and the whining wind. He began to wish fervently for daylight, yet he knew it was only just past midnight. Still, it was impossible to sleep. No matter which way he moved under the canvas, the wind always managed to whip rain over him. The best he could do for protection was to adjust the canvas so the water dribbled down his arm instead of his neck. There was only one good thing about the whole night; it was still sticky hot, and even soaking wet he was quite warm.

Once Tater moved restlessly as thunder sounded again. Apparently the rainstorm wasn't going to stop after all. Morgan stuck his head under one corner of the canvas shelter and out into the blinding night. It was a frightening sight. The wind wasn't so noticeably strong when he was huddled inside the boat, but it was blowing fiercely when he faced directly into it. He shined the lantern into the darkness. But the light only made it worse; it reflected the downpour in sharply slanting streaks of dull white, and he could see only a few yards. He heard the noisy *plop-plop* as the deluge hit the mud. There was still no water in the canal except for one tiny, rain-filled rivulet.

"You'd think all this rain would fill the canal to overflowing," he said grimly, as he ducked back under the tent. A sudden flash of lightning lit the boat brilliantly through the tarp. Then thunder rumbled out of the night, and it was followed by a sudden, heavier gust of wind that flapped the canvas violently.

"Wow!" He gulped. "That wind is really howling!"

Suddenly two lines snapped under the strain of the wind, and for a few hectic moments Morgan wrestled with the tarpaulin, pulling it back into place while still fighting with the upright as he tried to keep everything from toppling over on him. By the feel of it the wind was blowing at least thirty-five miles an hour, and probably more than that in the gusts. Lightning flashed and blinked the night briefly into light; thunder boomed. At last Morgan had the tarp tied down firmly, and again he peered back into the night through the poorly fitting side flaps. Another streak of lightning blinded him temporarily. Tater nuzzled his arm and cried nervously.

"I can't say I care for lightning bolts flashing all around myself," Morgan told the dog, as he struggled to lash a second line to the upright oar to keep it from bouncing from side to side unmanageably. He felt as if he were trying to hold down a kicking elephant.

Suddenly Morgan jerked upright to total attention. Tater was on his feet, too!

"It's a plane!" Morgan gasped.

Instantly he released the oar, and as he did it fell with a crash, the whole tarpaulin deflating on top of him in a flapping, wet mess. Morgan shoved the canvas aside, stumbled over Tater, and dived for the forward locker. He jerked open the door, pawed frantically through the contents, and found the case for the Very pistol. Dumping the metal box upside down, he snatched the gun and jammed the distress signal flares into his pocket. Then he vaulted over the rail of the boat and into the night.

He could see nothing but pouring rain, and he was able to judge the location of the canal banks only during each brilliant flash of lightning when the marsh was illuminated briefly. Nor could he hear the plane anymore; its sound was lost in the roar of the battering rain, the screaming wind, the wildly snapping, collapsed canvas shelter, and Tater's excited barks underneath it.

Morgan struggled up the high salt-marsh bank and came to a skidding halt. He leaned into the wind, and with the lantern handle held in his teeth he was able to see the fat-barreled gun in his hand. He snapped it open, shoved in a short, shotgunlike shell, then snapped the chamber closed.

Lightning jagged into the marsh ahead of him, and Morgan jerked backward terrified. But in those few moments before the cracking of thunder he heard the plane again. It was faint, but it was definitely a motor!

Morgan pulled back the hammer; the gun was stiff and unhandy, and getting it ready to fire was a slow process.

"Hurry!" he whispered to himself. "Hurry!" Then, finally, the gun was cocked. He held it in both hands over his head, pointed it into the air, and fired.

There was a sharp report, a small spout of flashing light, but at almost the same instant a brilliant blue-white streak of lightning bolted into the marsh grass in the near distance. In its light Morgan clearly saw the boat, the flapping tarpaulin, and Tater pulling and tugging as he tried to escape his restricting leash.

Furiously Morgan worked to open the gun, eject the shell, and insert another. He was working too slowly! But the gun was unfamiliar, and although he'd watched Father load it, it was the first time he'd ever used it himself. Thunder cracked; Morgan cringed violently from the deafening blast. But at last the gun was reloaded and he held it over his head. Yet before he could fire, another bolt of lightning jiggled into the ground beyond him and illuminated the world briefly. That time Morgan saw endless salt marsh; it was a silver-bluish green, windswept, lonely, and unfriendly.

"Blast this thunderstorm!" he muttered. "They won't be able to tell the flares from the lightning!" He pointed the gun into the air and fired. There was an instant report, another brief burst of light, and nothing more. If the distress flare had blossomed into further light overhead, it was out of his sight in the rain. Now he struggled furiously again to eject the spent shell. The gun wasn't easy to operate. He was not shooting the flares as quickly as they needed to be fired!

Morgan raised the gun again, but before he could fire lightning bolted into the ground right across the narrow canal. The lightning was too close! Quickly he pulled the trigger of the gun and shot the third shell, but at almost the same instant another streak of lightning flashed. Morgan stumbled down the bank and crouched in the mud. He put his arms over his head and huddled into as small a figure as he possibly could. He hated lightning! He hated thunder! He hated the wind and the rain! Home where it was warm and dry and safe. That's where he wanted to be. Yet miserable as he was, he remembered to check his pocket to see how many more flares he had left. Only two. He didn't dare fire the last ones until he was positive he heard the engine.

But the plane never returned. And it seemed another eternity before the main body of the thunderstorm passed over him. Then to Morgan's dismay, he realized the rain and the wind had not lessened in the least. He had to tie down the canvas tarpaulin quickly, or he was going to lose it.

Morgan got to his feet and staggered back to the boat. Tater was barking and yipping, and the moment the dog saw him appear out of the rain, he began to leap up and down nervously. Then, for an interminable time, Morgan wrestled with the snapping, flapping canvas. The vicious wind had given the wet material unbelievable power. Once a corner flipped out of his hand and flicked his arm like a whip. He jerked away from it, slipped, and fell in the mud painfully.

It soon became apparent that it was far too windy to use the oar to hold the tarpaulin upright, so Morgan did the next best thing. He lashed the canvas cover completely across both rails of the boat and over the bait barrel to give it sufficient height so the rain would run off it. Finally he was able to stumble inside the boat, and he pulled Tater in beside him. This time as Morgan took his position on the floorboards his head touched the wet, clinging tent top. He collapsed exhausted and breathed as if he had just run a fast mile.

He knew it must have been a Coast Guard rescue plane that had flown over him. Chances were very good Mother had called when he didn't come back. If the Coast Guard could locate Morgan by plane, they would be able to send help directly to him. But of all the times they could have flown over the boat the worst was during that lightning storm!

Morgan wiped his hand across his dripping, wet face, and then over the dial of his wristwatch in order to read it. One o'clock. It was time for the new weather report. He reached over Tater and inside the cuddy, where he exchanged the flare gun for the radio. He pulled up the antenna and flicked on the switch.

At that moment he discovered he was bleeding. That snapping canvas had cut him like a knife. He dabbed at the blood with a corner of the wet life jacket. As if to be of help, Tater swashed his tongue over the small wound.

"Thank you," Morgan said dryly, and then leaned back to rest. What was a piece of scraped skin compared to his uncomfortable bones. He felt bruised all over. Then he began to wonder if the plane would come back. If they knew he was stranded out here on the marsh, the chances were good that it would return.

Suddenly Morgan froze; the life jacket he had in his hand slipped through his fingers and fell to the floor beside him. He seized the radio with both hands.

"No," he whispered. "No! It can't be!"

He hadn't been paying attention to the radio weatherman's monotonous and factual report; he had been more concerned with his scratched arm and whether the airplane might return. But suddenly the words penetrated.

Morgan's face was white with shock. "It's turned. The hurricane has changed direction. It's heading straight for us!"

4
Lost

Morgan huddled over the radio again, protecting it from the driving rain, and listened to the report. The developing low-pressure area over Macon apparently had caused the hurricane to change course. It had turned; it was heading straight for land! Already the hurricane watch had been changed to a hurricane warning for his area. Repetitiously the weatherman explained that within six hours the storm was expected to hit the coast of South Carolina somewhere between Charleston and

Beaufort. Already Drum Island had reported the wind had switched to the east and was blowing steadily at forty-five miles an hour with stronger gusts.

"I have to get out of here!" Morgan whispered. Drum Island was practically right beside him! Then he bent his head intently over the radio again, sucking in his breath. The tide had started to come in at Drum Sound. Morgan's eyes lit up brightly. At last! The new wind direction was driving the water back into the flats. And that tide was going to be his salvation. Without it, he was stuck out on the marsh with no protection but the boat; with it, at least he had a chance to get to town before the worst hit.

Morgan pressed the radio against his ear in order to hear more clearly; it crackled with static. Apparently the extreme low water had stranded a lot of fishermen. All of Drum Island was completely isolated with the low tide. There were over a hundred people living on the island, and none of them were able to use their boats to get to town.

More rescue planes would be sent out. There were whole families on Drum Island. Timmy Haggerty lived there with about five brothers and sisters as well as his mother and father. And there were the Flemings; Lisa was in his class. At least he wasn't alone! Next time they all got together, what a tale they would have to tell. Morgan chewed at his lip uneasily.

There was one big problem. If all the people of Drum Island were in trouble, the planes and boats would rescue them instead of hunting for him. The evacuation of the island was naturally going to be first on everyone's mind. The whole island population would congregate at Taffy Hammock, since it was the most protected place, and the planes would go straight there and pick them up. Morgan swallowed. One stranded boy and one dog would be at the very bottom of the rescue list.

Morgan hunched up his shoulders. He was frightened, but he wasn't going to sit back and just give up. He could be a very stubborn human being when he put his mind to doing something. Morgan's eyes sparkled. He planned to get home all in one piece. He shook Tater sharply. "And then we're all going to Varnville to stay with Grandmother!" But Tater, huddled nervously against Morgan's leg, wasn't interested at all.

Since rescue was obviously going to be delayed,

Morgan began to look around carefully to see how best to help himself. The first thing was to start unloading everything he didn't need from the boat. Once the water started coming back into the canal, he wanted it to be as light as possible for rowing. That meant chucking out the bait barrel, the box of tools, and the picnic basket. Then he could get rid of one bucket, the extra crab-trap weights, and all that spare wire. Tater looked up and pushed his nose against his hand. For a moment Morgan stared at the dog.

"Don't worry, Tater, I'll save you. Now lie down. I know you want to reach high land."

The bait barrel was the heaviest object left in the boat, and rolling the unwieldy thing over the rail was a difficult chore. Next Morgan began to toss each small cement-block weight out into the night. He could barely hear them plop into the mud beside the boat over the noise of the pounding rain and howling wind. His eyes momentarily rested on the extra gas can. He shook his head. He must save that, and also the line, the anchor, and the life jacket. And he would have to put everything into the cuddy, otherwise it would all blow away. He also would have to save the rain slicker.

The material was very strong and would be excellent protection. To wear it would be terribly hot, but soon the wind would start screaming. When it did, he would rather be hot than have blowing marsh grass spearing him.

"How could such a beautiful day turn into such an unbelievable nightmare so quickly?" he said aloud. He ducked his head out into the rain-filled darkness. No water yet. He came back inside, dripping wet and windblown, and readjusted the canvas that had pulled loose at one end and had begun to flap wildly. Then he continued to toss outside the rest of the gear he had to leave behind. For a moment he considered leaving the motor, but rejected the idea. Somehow he must get that home and see that it was repaired for Father.

It was two o'clock when the water touched the boat. Tater heard it first. He was lying on the floorboards and leaning against the hull when suddenly he jerked upright and barked. He had heard the gurgling of the tide around the grounded boat's bottom next to his ear. Morgan snatched the light, pushed under the canvas, and looked at the canal.

"Water!" he yelled. "The tide's coming in!"

And it surely was coming fast. Already it bubbled around the discarded boat gear. He ducked back inside and looked over the boat once more. Except for the oars lying on the thwarts, the motor on the stern, and the two fuel cans, there was nothing in sight.

Morgan was upset by leaving the expensive gear behind, but there was no more time to think about that! He shook out his bright yellow foul-weather gear; it was time to put it on. In a few more minutes he would be ready to move the boat. Quickly he slipped into the trousers, pulled up the shoulder straps, and then shrugged into the jacket. Next he tied a large bandanna over his face to help take the sting out of that driving rain. He held up the life jacket. He could swim, but he knew he would be safer wearing it. Then he rigged a safety line around his waist. He would be tied securely to the bow so he wouldn't have to worry about losing the boat when he couldn't see it in the dark.

Turning to Tater, he slipped a line through his collar and then fastened it to one of the rings on his life jacket. "You'll be able to walk along the bank until we have enough water to row," Morgan said, as he rocked the boat back and forth by shifting his weight. The tide was coming in very fast. He tied the handle of the lantern to his jacket, and then he ran his tongue over his lips. Now he had to tackle the kicking elephant. The canvas cover had to come down and be stowed. He hated to see it go; it was good protection. Quickly he untied the lines in the stern, and he began to roll and fold the tarp forward with the wind.

How such lightweight canvas could become so powerful in the wind was difficult to understand. The tarpaulin began to flap violently, and the material jerked out of Morgan's hands with a crack. Instantly he lunged forward to get another grip on the material, but the edge of the canvas snapped and popped like a pistol firing. In desperation Morgan rolled over on top of the whole thing and tried to subdue the slippery monster long enough to get another firm hold. He couldn't manage it; the canvas slipped through his hands with another crack, the last lines snapped like threads, and within seconds the tarpaulin disappeared into the night.

Morgan collapsed against the rail, breathing heavily. The wind had settled that problem for him quickly enough. Then he leaned away from the wind and driving rain. How would he ever be able to drag the boat along in the shallow water toward Fancy Gap River? It was blowing so much that he could barely stand upright, and every bit of his exposed skin stung as if he were being pricked by pins. But somehow he climbed over the rail. Under no circumstances did he want to stay where he was!

Impatiently Morgan began to rock the boat from side to side. By now the water was over his ankles, but he kept sinking further and further into the mud. He rocked the boat again and again. It was nearly free. He helped Tater over the gunwale, and with one quick, affectionate pat on his back, he shoved the dog toward the invisible beach. Then Morgan slopped up to the bow, swung the line over his shoulder, and began to pull the boat.

Right away he felt it move slightly. The water was deep enough so that it should float at any instant, but the mud had formed a suction with the bottom, and the boat was being held firmly in place. Morgan closed his eyes and pulled furiously. He was never going to get out!

Ten minutes later the tide had risen well above his knees, and the boat floated. Morgan held his breath and stepped forward. At first the skiff inched ahead heavily, but then quite suddenly it moved more easily. He breathed in relief. He was on his way at last!

But Morgan's surge of elation didn't last long. It became almost impossible to keep his footing in the uneven holes that pitted the channel center. A few minutes later he was gasping for breath again. The rain poured down his face and ran into his eyes; he was unable even to see his hands holding tightly to the rope. Yet he kept on pulling as best as he could, knowing that every uneven, staggering step forward meant he was that much closer to home. And minute by minute the water kept rising and rising. Soon he would be able to row; then he would be able to go even faster.

What seemed to Morgan to be an eon later, he unexpectedly stepped into a very deep pit with his right foot. Instantly that leg sank into mud and water that came nearly to his hip. Frantically he struggled to pull himself up to firmer footing, and as he did he tried desperately to keep his balance. He couldn't do it! The pounding force of the wind, the heavy rain slicker and life jacket, and the boat drifting off to one side all worked against him. He toppled over into the water with a splash and floundered in the muddy shallows.

Quickly he rolled over and sat up, with the water lapping at his chin. The boat had grounded somewhere out of his sight at the end of his safety line, and he had to pull it back into the channel and start out all over again. Morgan struggled to his feet. He swung the line over his shoulder and stepped backward. At that instant he fell into water nearly over his head. Obviously the canal had considerable depth in midstream. He would finally be able to row!

Now he had to get Tater, but the dog refused to come to him. Slowly Morgan began to work his way to the end of Tater's leash. He couldn't see anything but sheets of rain, and he could barely open his eyes when he faced the wind. Suddenly he came to the end of the line, and his hands touched Tater. The dog was crouched on the mud trembling. Morgan took his collar and, by patting and coaxing, led him into the water.

It was as if he were blind. Morgan found his way back to the boat only by going hand over hand along his safety line, which was attached to the bow. When he bumped into the boat, where it had grounded against the bank, Morgan picked up Tater and shoved him on board. Then with a gigantic heave he pushed the boat into the channel. Swiftly Morgan slid over the rail, fumbled with the oars, and put them in their oarlocks. Yes, the water was deep enough for him to row! He struggled to position the boat where he thought midstream was located. He was only able to tell by the touch of the oar blades as the tips hit the bottom.

The crab boat had not been designed for rowing and in the wind and rain and utter darkness it proved very difficult. Yet Morgan tried his best. Every ounce of strength was important; every stroke was one more inch gained.

Before long the water rose sufficiently so that Morgan's blade tips no longer touched bottom. Though he could travel faster because of more power in his strokes, he was now unable to tell where he was going until he hit the mud of the extreme banks. Then he would swing the boat quickly and turn back to midchannel. All the time he was blindly groping his way. It soon became apparent that he was only guiding the boat in zigzags from bank to bank, and the wind and tidal current were what kept him moving forward steadily.

Almost an hour later Morgan stopped rowing. He sat up a little straighter and looked around him. He had made a slight turn, putting the wind directly behind him, but that was not what had caused him concern. Something was very wrong. He leaned over the rail of the boat and swished his hand in the water.

"Grass!" he gasped. But he couldn't be in marsh grass! He couldn't be! He squinted into the darkness. It had nearly stopped raining, and now he was able to see the boat completely. He also saw the reeds that brushed against the rail. It was plain that he had been blown out of the channel. Morgan ran his tongue over his lips. The water had risen over the edge of the canal, and he hadn't realized it. That was the reason the wind had felt stronger than ever the last few minutes. He was high enough now so that he was no longer being sheltered by the marsh banks.

For a moment Morgan considered continuing in the same direction he had been moving, but then he realized that was the most dangerous thing he could do. The wind was blowing him over the top of the marsh, and eventually it would take him straight into Drum Sound. But that huge body of water would be far too rough for his small boat! He needed to go any direction north of west to try to reach the high land of the mainland. If he didn't, he would be in trouble.

Morgan gave one light stroke on the oars to straighten the boat; then he climbed over the rail into the water. He would have to tow the skiff and try to find the canal again. Hoping he hadn't strayed too far away from it, he shined the light out ahead. Wherever the grass ended would indicate the canal's bank.

But it was no use. There was nothing in sight except a sea of partially submerged spartina. Morgan swallowed nervously. He could be anywhere! Slowly he began to guide the boat toward the northwest.

A half hour later he still hadn't found the canal. Morgan stopped walking and held the boat firmly to prevent it from blowing on ahead. That blinding rain had really confused him. He thought he had been staying in the channel, but all the time he must have been drifting over one of the marsh islands, and, worst of all, he didn't know for how long. He turned and faced into the wind as he tried to get his bearings. The wind was picking up tremendously, and he could no longer stand upright when he faced into it.

"At least it's stopped raining," he said to himself. The splatter he was getting was windblown spray; he could taste the salt. He flicked on the light, wiped his hand over his watch, and squinted at it. It would be light soon. He had better stay where he was and not wander around blindly. Come daylight he would be able to see where he was going. He dug out the anchor and tossed it over the side.

Since the rain had stopped, it was a good opportunity to set off a distress signal. If planes were heading out for Drum Island, they might see it. He had no intention of using the Very pistol; he had to save the two remaining flares until he definitely heard a plane. But he had an idea how he could make as much light as twenty flares.

Morgan leaned over the rail and removed the crab-buoy pickup hook from its rack by the wheel. He carried it a short distance away from the boat and painstakingly worked it into the water and marsh grass until it was standing upright. Then he came back, unscrewed the top of the portable gasoline can, and poured the contents into the tin bucket. There was a sudden, potent smell of raw gasoline.

Morgan then took the rag tied around the motor and squeezed the water out of it. Next he dipped it into the bucket of gasoline. He splashed back to the crab hook protruding out of the water, hung the bucket over the metal clip, and fixed the rag so that one part of it was in the gasoline and the remainder was hanging out of the bucket. Quickly Morgan rinsed his hands in the salt water; then he reached into his slicker pocket.

He held his breath as he struggled to ignite the protruding end of the gasoline-soaked rag, for it was very difficult to strike the waterproof matches in the wind and the wet. But the moment there was the slightest spark, the highly inflammable gasoline flashed, and almost instantaneously there was a heavy *hrummph* as the fuse ignited the bucket of gas explosively. Morgan leaped backward as flames flared far over his head. Then he returned to the boat. In the cuddy he had a plastic container of outboard motor oil. He unscrewed the cap and splashed back to his burning torch. Poured into the gasoline, the oil should keep the flare burning for a long time.

By five o'clock it began to grow light. No plane had come to investigate his windblown, flickering distress signal, and the water was rapidly rising. The tops of the spartina were nearly completely submerged, and the rising wind began to whip the water into sharp wavelets. Morgan knew the marsh grass would keep the wave action from building too steeply, yet, even so, the boat began to rock badly. And the deeper the water got, the larger those waves would become.

Suddenly a stronger-than-usual gust heeled the boat sharply to one side and to his dismay it blew over his still-flaring torch. The flames suddenly spread briefly over the water and then sputtered out. Morgan's heart sank, for the wind was too strong now to attempt to light another. But he was on his feet at once and ran to retrieve the bucket and crab hook before they disappeared under the water, and he carried them back to the boat. He climbed inside and huddled against the hull to listen to the latest weather report.

A few minutes later he clicked off the switch. Shakily he pushed down the antenna and carefully stowed the radio into the cuddy. He closed his eyes. It was blowing a sustained fifty-eight miles an hour at Drum Island with gusts of over sixty-five. The center of the hurricane was due to pass over the island in two hours, and they expected a rise in water of more than ten feet.

Morgan smashed his fist against the rail with such force it sounded as if he had driven it completely through the fiber glass. Tater leaped to his feet and jumped away from him.

Morgan leaned back against the boat's hull. He could feel the *bump-bump-bump* of the bottom as the boat jerked up and down over the waves.

He knew now that he would never reach Suggs Mill. There wasn't enough time; he would be forced to endure the full brunt of the hurricane lost in the middle of the marsh. A great wave of hopelessness washed over him. Tater's and his chances of ever seeing the end of this day alive were almost nonexistent.

5
Hammock Haven

Morgan opened his eyes in a few moments. It was becoming quite light, but from where he crouched on the floorboards, all that he could see were the scudding, dark clouds streaking past overhead. They were low, threatening, and ugly. He got to his knees and squinted at the world beyond the rail of the boat. There was nothing in sight but choppy, whitecapped water and an occasional patch of barely visible marsh-grass tops. So much spray was being flung ahead of the wind that he could not see far; there certainly was no sign of Suggs Mill. For a moment he wondered if perhaps the town had been inundated in the same high water that covered the marsh, yet he knew that would not be likely. At least, it couldn't have happened yet. He cupped his hands around his eyes, pulled the bandanna as high as possible to protect his face from the peppering wind-flung spray, and stared into the wind. To the east was the black of darkest night, yet it was from that direction the sun was bringing the dawn. So far, however, not the slightest trace of light showed there, except for an occasional flash of lightning.

Tater whined, and Morgan turned toward him with a frown. As he did, he sucked in his breath with a startled gasp.

Looming out of the sheets of blowing spray was one of the hammock islets, and the dog was watching it with interest.

"I don't know where I am," Morgan complained. There was no high land around the canal! He wondered if he could have been blown completely over Fancy Gap River and not realized it. He ran his tongue over his lips, unnerved by the thought, and squinted into the gray, windswept gloom. It was definitely one of the tiny, high islands that sparsely dotted the tidelands. They weren't really high he knew; they were only a few feet more in elevation than the marsh itself, yet they had one impressive distinction. Nature had left beneath those tiny hammocks firm ground with sufficient earth and sustenance to support a small amount of sturdy, green growth.

Morgan shaded his eyes from the flying spray. It was difficult to see how big it was. Some of the hammocks were not much larger than an oversized house; others were three or four times that size. Then for a brief moment the spray cleared slightly.

"That's a pine tree!" Morgan yelled suddenly. He leaped to the stern and began pulling in the anchor, and within moments he began to row.

His enthusiasm was infectious; Tater clambered up to the bow and stood in his favorite riding spot with his ears blowing straight out in the wind. As they came closer to the hammock, the dog began to bark. Morgan's spirits soared. The little island wasn't Suggs Mill, but at that particular moment it seemed a near heaven. He kept snatching glances over his shoulder, afraid somehow that what he saw was only a figment of his imagination, and that if he didn't keep it in sight, it would disappear as if by magic.

The wind was directly behind the boat, and he was traveling fast. He would have to circle around and land on the lee side. Tater bustled back, skidded up on the seat beside him, shoved his nose into his face, and barked again.

Morgan laughed; things were looking up at last. Then the hammock was alongside. His oars hit bottom as the water shoaled, and he quickly turned along the shoreline.

"It's high!" Morgan shouted. He had caught sight of knobby land among the fringe of thick brush that beat and thrashed in the wind.

He cut in and began to row violently to bring the boat into the shelter of the island. Then he was in the lee, the wind slackened, the boat turned easily upwind, and he hit bottom with a crunch. Tater leaped over the side, and Morgan jumped out beside him into water ankle-deep. He pulled the boat farther ashore and found himself standing on a gravelly shell beach instead of mud.

"Wow!" he said. "Look at that!"

He faced at least five pine trees; one of them was big and heavy and looked very old. "And there's an oak! We're in luck!" Morgan patted Tater vigorously; the dog was suddenly frisky and excited. Morgan unsnapped his safety line from the bow and ran to tie the boat securely to a small cedar. Then he looked around thoughtfully.

He was certain that it wasn't Razor Back Hammock. It was much too small. Morgan looked at the trees. They were thrashing nearly as violently as the brush. Branches had been toppled from higher up, and they were strewn here and there along the tiny beach. He would have to watch out for more falling limbs.

It was wonderful to be able to stand upright and not be doubled over by the ferocity of the wind. The protection given by the brush and trees was phenomenal. And for the first time in hours, he didn't have to bellow at Tater to be heard.

"This is great!" he said enthusiastically. He wished it was Suggs Mill, but it would have to do. He stared out beyond the hammock. It was growing quite light in the west, and he could see better than ever. But there was only water in sight; the spartina had totally disappeared under the rising tide. Morgan felt his elation ebb. Never before had he seen all the marshlands submerged. Normally the hammocks were only brushy, tree-covered dots in fields of grass. Now his newfound island was isolated in a vast sea. Whitecaps and flying spray had turned the world a misty gray white. The idea of getting into the boat and intentionally going back into that turbulence in order to try to find town was the most depressing thought in the world. No, he would not go out there again!

Then Morgan began to explore the small hammock, and as he rounded the eastern side, the wind hit him with such tremendous violence that he staggered backward away from it. He gripped Tater's collar and dragged the dog back toward the protective lee. "We must keep away from that wind!"

But Tater tugged at his leash impatiently. Morgan shook his head. "No, we must stay tied together. If one of those stronger gusts catches you, it could blow you off the hammock entirely, and you might not be able to swim back. Come on, let's have a look and see how high the elevation is mid-island." He pushed back the brush and started to step through to the center of their islet.

Suddenly the greenery in front of him thrashed more violently than ever. Morgan jumped back away from it, and he crashed into Tater, nearly knocking him to the ground. A great blue heron erupted out of the bushes right in front of Morgan's face. But once in the open the bird was caught by the wind, and it was swooped in a circle out of control. As it turned its powerful wings whacked Morgan on the head and bent him to his knees. Then the bird crashed back into the brush and disappeared.

"For crying out loud!" Morgan exclaimed, as he got to his feet. "Apparently we aren't the only refugees from the storm on this hammock."

The small island, no more than fifty yards across, was surrounded with a fencelike wall of small trees and bushes well over ten feet high. Once he started off again and pushed through this shrubbery, Morgan was instantly in the island's center. Under the pines and the lone oak tree was a small clearing with a few palmettos growing as low ground cover. As he looked around the edges of this tiny open space he spotted more birds in the brush, most of them egrets and herons. They were very still and stared out intently at them from their refuges in the leaves. Nervous as the birds were made by the presence of the new shelter-seek-

ing arrivals, they all remained exactly in place. Instinct seemed to have warned them that flying was dangerous. Protected though it was in midhammock, the wind was still blowing small twigs and greenery constantly from the higher branches, and they littered the ground. Only when something fell with a crash beside them did the birds move. Then they flapped quickly to another sheltered place and resettled with their backs to the blasting wind.

Quickly Morgan put his hand on Tater's muzzle to keep him from barking and frightening them. If any of the birds attempted to leave the hammock in this wind, they would be killed. But Tater had rapidly lost interest in nearly everything. He too was concerned only with keeping his back to the vicious gusts, for moment by moment the wind was increasing.

Morgan looked at one very large tree limb that obviously had just fallen. The split inner wood shined brightly in the poor light. He looked overhead and saw the jagged scar on the oak tree where the heavy branch had been ripped from the main trunk. He could also see more birds; they were huddled behind nearly every shielded spot on every tree. They looked windblown and defenseless as they clutched the branches, and they swayed precariously on their long pipestem legs.

Morgan led Tater to a shelter behind one of the islet's small cedars, which gave some protection from the wind, and wondered if the inner part of the tree might offer them even more protection. He pulled the tightly packed foliage apart and peered inside to see if there was sufficient room for a boy and a dog.

There was a sudden chattering of disturbed small birds, and he realized that the cedar's inner branches were crowded with red-winged blackbirds. They flittered and jittered about nervously until Morgan dropped the limbs back into place and left them all safely tucked inside their cedar blanket.

Suddenly Morgan sucked in his breath sharply. Water! Since he had pushed into the hammock's center, the tide had risen until now it glistened along the bases of the low bushes. He could hear the swash of the waves, hitting the shell beach just beyond, and it sounded loud even over the scream of the wind in the trees. He wished the hammock was a hundred times larger and higher in elevation. The tops of the trees were at least forty feet high, and the ocean could never cover the hammock entirely, but obviously the tide was going to rise further. He had better start to prepare for it. First he would—

Morgan's thoughts dwindled off. His attention turned to the lip of water beginning to trickle toward him from the east. Just ahead of it scurried a raccoon, which must have been flooded out of its hiding place in the brush. The little humpbacked animal shot him one hasty glance from its bandit face as it darted in front of his feet before disappearing into the thick fronds of the palmettos.

Another fugitive from the storm! Morgan swallowed nervously. How small his island seemed all of a sudden. The five pines and the oak were scantily branched and vulnerable. He began to visualize the rising water engulfing the hammock's fringe of brush and finally rising mercilessly over the tips of the short cedars. He knew that such a thing could happen.

Every ounce of optimism and well-being vanished that instant. Morgan shuddered. He wasn't safe after all. He stared at the water that had begun to lap at the toes of his sneakers and stepped backward away from it. As he did a gust hit him with a tremendous blast and rocked him on his feet. The wind was increasing in strength beyond belief.

Morgan turned back to the boat. He had to bring it here into the center of the hammock before the wind made up any more. The pine would be his home base. He thumped the largest tree with his fist as he passed it. He would have preferred the oak as his defense against the wind, as its roots were probably the deepest, but he didn't care for the looks of it. It was wormy up there, and rot had worked at that toppled limb. He didn't want to end up caught under a downed tree.

Morgan began to unpack the boat completely. It had to be as light as possible in order for him to move it across the beach. The job didn't take him long; he hadn't that much gear left. In minutes he had carried everything to the tree except for the outboard. And Morgan realized now he would have to get rid of the motor; it was only dead weight. He ran his tongue over his lips, stonily wrenched the engine off the transom, and let it fall into the water with a splash. Slowly, inexorably, he was being deprived of his possessions. Would the time soon come, he wondered, when everything would be gone, including himself?

Morgan gritted his teeth. He planned on putting up a stiff fight for his life. His odds were not very good at that moment, but there was one thing he had that the storm didn't have: brains. He might not be able to outrun the hurricane, but he sure enough could try to outthink it.

Morgan bent his head to protect it from the driving wind and the pelting of the wind-stripped, blowing leaves. He had to get the boat through the brush and to that pine!

The job turned out to be quite easy, because by then the water had risen to the point where the boat floated anywhere on the hammock. All he needed to do was push the shrubs apart and pull it to the base of his chosen pine tree. Then he reloaded the boat. As he put the Very pistol case back inside the cuddy locker, he decided to keep the gun in his belt and the flares in his pocket. It was the one thing he might need quickly.

And there was that raccoon again! As Morgan leaned against the tree and tried unsuccessfully to get some protection from the wind, he watched the animal. Knowing Tater's love for the chase, he glanced at the dog. But Tater appeared uninterested. He was crouched against the tree with his head down, silently suffering the lashings of the whipping leaves of the nearly submerged palmettos beside him.

The raccoon was having a hard time, for it had no place left to go. It was too windy to climb one of the trees, and Morgan watched the frantic animal splash from place to place through the rising water as it tried desperately to find higher land. Finally, in near exhaustion, it struggled to a small, sturdy bush still above the surface, and there it wedged itself into a crotch of two limbs. A little blue heron had found shelter there too, and it instantly was obvious that there was not going to be sufficient room for them both. The raccoon raised its head and showed its teeth viciously at the bird. But the heron was not at all frightened; it arched its long neck and pecked the raccoon painfully with its sharp beak. The animal squealed piercingly and leaped back into the water. Trembling helplessly and neck-deep in the rising tide, it once more began to look around for another safe haven. For a long few moments, its alert, dark eyes studied the two outsiders huddled beside the big pine. Then, as if making a final choice between life and death, the raccoon waded toward them, jumped up to the rail of the boat, and then flopped down on the floorboards in the bow.

Morgan sighed. He had to get Tater in there too. He lifted the dog into the stern and wondered briefly if the two animals would tolerate each other so close together. But the storm had made them conscious only of survival. They totally ignored one another.

Crab-fashion, Morgan began to inch sideways to the eastern edge of the hammock. He wanted to take one good look in that direction now that it was fully light. However, he could not stand up straight when he faced the full blast of the storm even in the lee of the trees. He was forced to clutch the thrashing branches of the cedars to help pull himself along. As he did, one tree suddenly leaned toward him precariously. The rising water had loosened its roots, and with his strong tug for support the tree was no longer able to withstand the force of the driving wind. It fell with a crash and a splash beside Morgan's feet. Small birds like stuffed toys were thrown into the water. Some splashed with wildly flapping wings to the next cedar; a few were caught in the branches and disappeared in the waves; others were whipped out of sight in the violent wind to their deaths. Another gust caught him unexpectedly, and Morgan lunged forward and gripped another tree. If he had not held on tightly, he too would have been blown downwind much like the birds.

Morgan cupped his hands around his eyes and stared into the tempest. Savage, turbulent, black clouds whirled toward him, and the trailing, raging tendrils of scud were so low hung that they raced through the upper branches of the trees. Knee-high waves were breaking on the shallows, and the foam from the surf had blown into the windward brush, giving it a cotton-coated look. Morgan knew that once the water rose over the hammock's outer fence of bushes, the entire island would be swept with those same waves. There was not the slightest sign the water was abating; it was growing deeper and deeper. Nor was the wind lessening; it was becoming stronger and stronger.

Morgan had to turn away; he could no longer stand the pain of the stinging, windswept spray, and it was even difficult to breathe. But as he turned he caught sight of another, even worse, menace. For a brief moment he stood hypnotized with horror. Then he closed his eyes. What he saw was imprinted upon his mind forever.

Driving relentlessly toward him and standing out

stark-white against the black cloud bank as it waved and undulated like a ghostlike dancer was a waterspout.

This was the end. Morgan was positive no one could live through the holocaust of a tornado with only a low, swamped island for protection.

6
Trapped

Morgan came out of his despair with a jolt. When he had seen the waterspout, he felt utter hopelessness, but he knew that to save his life he must do everything possible to prepare for its approach. He turned and ran back to the boat.

He had to secure an extra line to the stern. First he snatched the nylon off the thwart and splashed the rope to the pine and then back again. Next he worked furiously to make fast the anchor rode to a protruding tree root. There was another line in the cuddy; it would make the second stern line. Quickly he secured them, and minutes later he had the boat tied with so many lines it looked like a fly caught in a giant spider's web.

Finished, he had to climb away from the water. He reached above his head, hooked one leg over a branch, and then swung himself completely up. The tree swayed and thrashed so violently in the wind he could barely hold on to it. As he lashed his safety line to the tree's main trunk, he shot one look at Tater. The dog was in the boat; he was going to have to weather the waterspout there. Morgan kept his head down and hung on tightly. The closer the tornado came to him, the more the wind was going to increase.

Yet it didn't seem possible the wind could blow as strongly as it did. Morgan wrapped his arms tightly around the tree, pressing himself like a leech against the bark. He felt as if he were riding an enraged bucking horse. His clenched fingers were sticky with the sap that oozed from the tree's trunk, and he smelled the sharp pungency of pitch pine.

Here it came! There was a tremendous roaring of noise. Rain suddenly poured over him as if he were beneath a gigantic waterfall. There was an explosive crack, a whistling, tearing, and groaning. The tree shook and throbbed, and if Morgan had not been tied to it, he never would have been able to withstand such a heaving, violent motion. Debris began to crash down on his back with heavy, jolting thuds, and somewhere overhead a limb split and fell and narrowly missed him as it whirled off beyond his head.

Then, abruptly, it stopped raining. The tree jerked itself back upright. Spray still pelted him like needles; the wind still screamed and shrieked; but the momentary violence of the passing waterspout had abated.

Cautiously Morgan looked up. He was no more than a few inches from the tree, yet as he blinked away the water that poured down his face, he could barely believe his eyes. It was unbelievable, but between himself and the pine was a fish. Its mouth was slightly open, and it was a wet, slippery silver. Its gills opened and closed in quick, sharp movements, so it was alive.

"It's a mullet," Morgan said stupidly.

Then as if to prove it was not a vision, the fish suddenly began to flap furiously. Instantly Morgan was forced to lunge backward to protect himself from the smacking tail and sharp fins. The mullet was slick and slimy, and a hectic few moments went by before he was able to grab it behind the gills. Quickly he tossed it over his shoulder, and it disappeared downwind. But no sooner had the first mullet disappeared than another one crashed down on top of him. It slithered across his back and disappeared below him, while yet another thrashed down through the tree limbs and smacked him on the shoulder.

"It's raining fish!" he bellowed. The waterspout must have picked up a school of mullet and then dropped them as it jumped over the hammock.

He looked up. Mullet were everywhere! They dotted the pine from top to bottom like silver ornaments. Some were falling from the heights into the water while others were flapping helplessly as they were caught and wedged between branches and limbs. But he had no more time to gape at misplaced fish.

"Tater!" he screamed. The violence of the wind had capsized the boat; it was upside down! Morgan untied his safety line and was on the move. He slipped over the windblown branch and held him-

self suspended from it for a moment as he tried to decide on the safest place to leap. There wasn't any; he jumped anyway. In a matter of minutes the water had risen over his head, and he had to swim, pushing limbs and brush apart as he went.

But Tater was all right! As Morgan plunged and swam through masses of fallen branches and uprooted bushes, he saw the flash of brown paws. Morgan splashed up beside the boat, but as he did a sudden gust of wind sent a wave straight into his face. By the time he could breathe and see again, he realized he was being swept away. Wildly he clutched for the stern as he went by, missed, and then his hand touched Tater. The dog had seen him coming and swum to meet him. Morgan snatched Tater's collar and held on tightly. Slowly they worked their way backward until, at last, Morgan was able to get a firm grip on the sharp skeg on the boat's bottom.

For a moment Morgan rested and breathed thankfully. If Tater hadn't come to him a second ago and helped him swim back, he would have been lost forever. But now he must turn the boat over. Tater had no place to stand up; he was being forced to swim continually.

Morgan knew if he pulled on the boat's opposite rail and at the same time stood on the skeg, the skiff would roll right side up. But the boat was rolling and wallowing in the water like a skittish whale. The screaming wind constantly shoved him off balance as he tried to get a foothold on the slippery fiber glass. Time and again he was thrown face down in the water. Finally he was able to get into position with his hands on the gunwale. He lunged backward and at the same time pushed his feet on the keel with his full weight. The boat tipped, almost instantly the wind caught the exposed surface, and it teetered up on its side. An oarlock dangled from its socket over Morgan's head. He snatched it quickly and pulled violently. With this added weight, the boat suddenly flipped over with a gigantic splash.

But it was full of water up to the rail, and Morgan stared at it helplessly. Worse yet, he looked anxiously at the two lines that secured it to the pine tree. All the rest of his ropes had snapped and broken in the wind. Morgan knew that if those last thin pieces of nylon parted, the boat would be swept away from the hammock. There was nothing to stop it. The protective fringe of brush that surrounded the islet had disappeared almost completely.

Morgan turned to Tater and helped him into the boat. Though neck-deep, the dog at last was able to stand up. But it was an unsteady refuge for him, as his weight made the waterlogged boat lurch in the wind and waves and come precariously close to capsizing again.

Later Morgan would have to bail it out. Now he had to tie the boat more securely before he lost it. He gathered together all the broken lines he could find and lashed them around the pine. Adjusting the new ropes was a difficult and time-consuming task, and after that he struggled with the boat and heaved it up against the tree trunk. Morgan had lost his protective bandanna at some point, and he was forced to suffer through the spray and pine needles that lashed at his exposed face. When finally he had the boat firmly in place once more, he realized he had scraped his knuckles, and they were bleeding. But there was no time to worry over bruised fingers. He turned back to Tater and the swamped boat.

He could not reach the bucket in the forward cuddy, so Morgan began to remove the water by using his slicker hat as a bailing tin. But before long he had to stop. He fell forward and leaned his forehead against the rail of the boat, exhausted. He nearly had reached the end of his strength. Nothing could be worse than his position. He was marooned in a thrashing pine tree, the wind was blowing over eighty miles an hour, he was being beaten brutally by flying branches and whipping leaves, and he was nearly drowning in spray and water. Yet Morgan's eyes sparkled. He was still alive; that in itself was an amazing fact! It gave him new heart.

For a minute longer Morgan rested and stared out at the world downwind of him. Now that he took the time, he saw that in the violence of the waterspout's passing, the oak tree had toppled over completely. Fortunately, he had not chosen it for his refuge, for it lay in a jumble of spikelike, broken branches that were heavily awash in the waves. One of the smaller pines had partially fallen too. It was leaning at so severe an angle that its topmost branches splashed in the water. Nearly all of the cedars were underwater, and there was no sign of the birds. Morgan closed his eyes and swallowed painfully. In the horror of those few moments they must have been all blown out of the trees. Morgan picked up his hat and went back to bailing.

Ten minutes later the boat was cleared of water, and what spray splashed into it easily drained off through the scuppers in the bilge. Tater had found a protective lee and was lying tightly wedged between a thwart and the hull. Occasionally a pine cone or torn greenery clattered down onto the floorboards alongside of him, but Tater never moved. Morgan knew that the dog was as tired as he was.

And there was another problem. Downwind was the raccoon. Morgan thought the animal had been killed when the boat had capsized, but he was wrong. Somehow the animal had escaped, and now it clutched the very top of the one still-exposed cedar tree. This was its last hold on life. The water was rising, and within minutes it was going to be swept away and into that endless expanse of wind-whipped waves beyond him. Yet Morgan could see no possible way he could rescue the animal. Though the distance to the raccoon was not far downwind, to swim the animal back to the boat was totally impossible, even if the raccoon would tolerate human interference in its predicament. Nor was it able to swim the distance upwind to the boat and battle the wind and waves on its own. Morgan didn't know what to do. He couldn't just sit and watch the helpless animal be washed away to its death.

Finally he removed his life jacket and coiled the safety line that was attached to it. For a moment he stared at the stranded animal. He judged its distance from his own refuge on a limb in the lee of the tree trunk beside the boat. Then quickly Morgan heaved the jacket downwind as far as he could. It landed with a splash and began to drift away from him.

Morgan sat up a little straighter. He jerked the attached safety line and guided the direction of the jacket's drift. The orange material was very bright, but he wondered if the raccoon had a sense of color and if so, could it recognize its last chance for survival floating toward it. Morgan tugged the line a bit more; the life belt swung closer to the cedar.

"It's coming right for you," he said carefully, as if he expected the animal to be listening to him. He held his breath; the makeshift rescue raft had bumped into the cedar branches. It was a perfect landing. Obviously the raccoon had seen it coming;

it sharply eyed the life jacket from its wet and windy perch.

"Just leave that tree," Morgan said, as the life belt touched the raccoon's side. It had drifted into a perfect position for the animal to reach. Carefully Morgan took up the line; he tried to hold the life jacket in place, but the wind and waves were working against him. Slowly it began to drift away. The raccoon turned slightly and watched it float off.

Then, when Morgan was sure it was too late, the

animal suddenly sank into the water and began to swim toward the jacket.

"Grab it, man!" Morgan gasped.

The raccoon pawed at the canvas material as it tried to climb on top of the unstable raft, but its footing slipped and it splashed underwater. When it surfaced, the animal frantically pawed for another grip and finally managed to hook a claw through one of the jacket's metal rings. With its teeth it began to snap at the shoulder padding, caught a

grip, and held on, while with the other paw it snagged a dangling strap of webbing. Immobile, the raccoon held on for its life.

Morgan began to pull in the line that was attached to the jacket. Slowly the improvised rescue craft came toward him, towing its small survivor. But the raccoon did not attempt to leap for the rail of the boat when finally it bumped alongside the hull. It refused to release its grip on the bobbing raft. Yet obviously it could not stay where it was for long. In desperation, Morgan began to tow the animal straight to his side.

He ran his tongue over his lips as the raccoon fidgeted nervously. Then it was within reach! Quickly Morgan lifted both the jacket and the animal out of the water in one gigantic scoop. Before the raccoon realized what had happened, it was safely inside the boat. It tumbled head over heels onto the floorboards and crashed to a stop against Tater. There was a sudden flurry of frightened, wet animals as they leaped apart and lunged in opposite directions. The trembling raccoon dived under the forward thwart, while Tater scuttled terrified into the stern.

At that moment it happened. While Morgan put

on his life jacket again and breathed in relief at the successful rescue, the shrieking, howling, whining wind began to stop blowing. Morgan froze as if he had been turned to stone. For the first time in hours he could face the east. He heard the roar of surf breaking over the downed oak and the *crack-crack* of waves as they beat against the boat's bottom.

"The eye," Morgan whispered. "It's the eye of the hurricane!"

Suddenly he came back to life. Furiously he untied the lines on the boat that only minutes before he had struggled with such difficulty to secure.

Hurry! He had to hurry! He jerked the boat forward as he tried to pull it around to the other side of the tree. It caught on a submerged, broken branch and stuck fast. He floundered back through the water, swam to the bow, and began to guide it around the obstruction. "I'm in the very center of the storm!" Morgan gasped. He had to work faster! He jerked the boat through the ugly, protruding limbs. With his foot, he shoved the boat away from a cracked branch and began to tie lines like a demon. Then he yanked the bow around another part of the fallen oak. He secured the stern line around a branch to his left. Ducking under another limb, he tied the boat to yet another tree.

Morgan was gasping for breath. Never had he worked so fast or so hard. He shot a quick glance at the eastern horizon. At last the ugly, black wall of darkness had lightened. He could see blue sky!

Quickly he tied another line to the bow. How much time did he have? Five minutes? Ten? He splashed back alongside the boat and carefully began to check each knot. He had managed to move the boat completely around the tree, and he had tied it securely. Tater became aware of the change in the weather; he put both feet on the rail and looked out.

"Get back down inside! This calm isn't going to last!" Morgan snapped, and he cuffed Tater on the chin. Startled, the dog dropped back to the bottom of the boat, out of sight.

Morgan looked up as he retied a knot double hard. The sun was coming out, and the world momentarily took on sparkling color. The waves were dazzling in vivid blue and turquoise and snowy white, the trees gleamed in all shades of greens, and the clouds glowed intensely in luminous black and gray and yellow.

Morgan began to gather up his safety line. It was going to blow harder than ever in a few minutes, and the wind would blow out of the west. Where he had been protected before, he would now be endangered. He wrenched his eyes away from a world of colors that seemed too brilliant to be real and started to climb onto the limb next to the trunk. It would be in the lee. He dared not risk getting into the boat; it might capsize again. He must also watch that leaning pine tree when the wind hit. It was tipped toward him, but he couldn't do much about it, and there was no place left for him to go.

Nor was Morgan at all certain he could endure the same sort of horror all over again. For when the wind struck once more, not only was it going to come from the opposite direction, it was going to hit him with as much force as before. It would be worse than ever for him, because it would come in one terrible gust. He pulled himself up to the branch of the tree that would provide his new protection.

"I wish it was over," he said aloud. But he knew it wasn't; he was going to get a blast of wind that would rock him unmercifully. He lashed a line around his waist, and he started to wrap it around the trunk to tie himself securely in place.

But he didn't have time. For at that moment, the hurricane struck again. The wind hit him with every bit as great a force as before, and it came with a roaring of tremendous, raging noise. And as he expected, it came out of the west, where, until that moment, he had found shelter and safety.

Morgan felt as if he had been hit with a gigantic club. The sudden blast of wind threw him forward, and since his safety line was not tied securely, he pitched into the boat in front of him with a crash. As he fell, he saw the leaning pine falling toward him. It crashed into the water only feet away and forced a towering wall of water upward. Seconds later the wave hit the boat with a crash. Lines snapped, the boat swamped, and then it turned turtle.

Morgan thrashed for his life, as he tried to swim out from under the boat that had started to come down on top of him. But the tremendous roll had thrown Tater forward and straight into him. Frantically Morgan struggled to push the dog aside. Then Tater found footing and was able to leap clear, but by then it was too late for Morgan. The boat came down over his head, and he was shoved deep underwater.

Fortunately, Morgan had managed to get a good gulp of air, and he kicked furiously as he attempted to reach the surface. Almost instantly his head bumped against a solid, wide, immovable obstruction, and he knew at once that it was the inside floorboards. He splashed violently lunging from one side to another as he tried to find a way to escape. Then, miraculously, he was able to surface. He groped with his hands over his head and touched the rough bilgeboards; then his eyes focused blearily on the cavernous gray world that was the interior of the capsized boat. He had managed to come up in a tiny bit of air space that had been caught in the bow. But he could not stay where he was; there was barely space for his eyes, nose, and mouth. He sucked in one great lungful of air, and he dived.

Blindly he began to feel his way toward the place where he knew the rail of the boat was located. He touched the hull. He found the rail! Gripping it with both hands, he pulled himself deeper underwater. He had to get beneath the side of the boat before he could resurface outside in clear water.

Now his air was running out! Frantically Morgan pulled; he tried to go farther down. He wasn't deep enough yet to swim under the rail.

Then his life jacket caught on a snag, and he was jerked to a stop. He was trapped!

7
Sharpshooter

As he forced himself to hold his breath for a few last seconds, Morgan jerked forward with every ounce of his strength. He had to free his life jacket from the snag before he could slip below the rail to safety. He yanked again, again, and then something ripped. The next moment he squirmed under the side of the boat and popped to the surface in open water. He gulped in great, sobbing lungfuls of air. He was alive! He was out from beneath the overturned boat.

Morgan looked up. Ugly, overcast skies once more had settled over the hammock. He was surrounded by tangled branches of downed pine trees, and as the wind whipped the greenery against his skin, he flinched away from it in spasms of pain. He put his back to the screaming wind and tightly gripped the keel of the boat beside him. As he did, he saw that the falling tree not only had swamped and rolled over the boat, it had sent a spear-shaped splinter of wood completely through the fiber-glass stern.

Morgan looked quickly to his other side. The raccoon was not more than twenty feet away from him, wallowing heavily in the water as it clutched a thrashing, fallen branch with its forepaws.

Then Morgan sobbed in relief. There was Tater! The raccoon had shifted its position slightly, and as it did, Morgan had a better view of the dog. Immediately Morgan realized that Tater was in trouble. The dog's face was inches from the water, and though he struggled to stay above the surface, wave after wave plunged him under completely. He was partially caught beneath the branches of a fallen tree!

Without a moment's hesitation, Morgan left the

small protection the overturned boat gave him and began to swim toward Tater. Yet reaching him was going to be a difficult, if not an impossible, task. Not only did he have to swim upwind, he had to face a dense maze of broken branches. He made poor progress as he lurched over the top of the limbs, and the wind buffeted him with such fury that he was continually thrown backward.

Breathless, Morgan finally stopped. He caught a handful of pine needles, and he looked around for an easier passageway to the dog. There was none! Yet he had to reach Tater! If one of those waves kept him underwater longer than he could hold his breath, the dog would drown.

Quickly Morgan decided what had to be done. He slipped off his life jacket, tied it to his belt, and let it float behind him. He had no intention of leaving it, but he could no longer wear it. Its life-saving flotation was working against him. Next he slipped off his heavy slicker pants and then his jacket to lighten his weight.

At once the whipping pine needles lashed at his exposed arms and neck, and he gritted his teeth against the pain. Still, he carefully rechecked the route he had to take to reach Tater. Then he sucked in a deep breath, submerged, and began to swim underwater toward him. Beneath the surface the horrendous noise of the hurricane was replaced with a bubbling, dull murmur. When he had to come up for air, he clutched a limb to keep himself from being thrown backward by the wind; then he drew in another long breath, plunged under, and started off. Promptly he hit a submerged branch with a painful crack, but he ducked sideways, slipped under it like a fish, and then resurfaced.

Already he had come a considerable distance. Had he been swimming on top of the water, the wind and waves would have hindered him badly; underwater there was nothing to impede his progress except the frustrating jumble of broken limbs. Again and again he dived to evade them and swam on.

He surfaced the final time beside the raccoon, which was holding on tightly to the branch for survival, and, for a brief second, their eyes met. But Morgan quickly turned to Tater.

The dog was in a bad position. Morgan could see right away that his safety line was what was pinning him down. It was caught somewhere underwater. Worst of all the limb that had made him a helpless prisoner also was supporting most of his weight, and in every gust of wind the branch heaved up and down violently, throwing Tater down into the water. During those moments no amount of pulling, tugging, and lurching kept him on the surface. The dog had to use every ounce of his strength to get air to breathe.

Quickly Morgan pulled his trailing life jacket to his side, and he adjusted it carefully under Tater's muzzle. It raised the dog's face out of the water a small amount, but not nearly enough. On top of everything else, the tide was still rising. He had to free Tater instantly!

It should have been simple enough to do. Earlier Morgan had tied a section of nylon line to the dog's chain collar, but when the dog had been thrown out of the boat, the pressure apparently had jammed the knot. Now as Morgan tried to release the knot, he realized he would have to cut it with a knife. And he didn't have one! It was somewhere under the capsized boat. Nor could he remove Tater's collar and set the dog free. The mass of line had jammed the snap on the metal chain! Morgan would have to free the other end of the leash that was caught somewhere under the surface.

Morgan released the branch and dived. It was difficult to see in the foam and bubbles and moving pine needles, yet he finally made out the white blur of the rope. He followed with his hands along the slick nylon until he touched an immense piece of wood that appeared to be the trunk of a tree. Then he felt another smaller limb, which was bent in a sharp V-shape. Tater's line was caught between these two sections as if in a vise. It was as strong as iron; Morgan couldn't budge it an inch!

Now his time was up; his air was running out. He came to the surface just as Tater was being forced underwater by the heaving limb, despite the protective life jacket supporting his face. Morgan heard the dog's ragged gasps for breath above the screaming wind. Quickly he put both hands around Tater's head and pulled him up out of the water. Tater was choking, gagging, coughing, but finally he caught a ragged breath.

Morgan had to release the end of that line immediately! But to do so he needed something with which to pry the two tree sections apart. Then he felt a surge of sudden relief. One of the oars had been thrown out of the boat when it rolled over, and it was wedged under a limb beside the raccoon.

As he swam to get it, he knew when he removed the oar that the stranded animal was going to lose its precarious footing. But it couldn't be helped; Tater was more important. Yet as Morgan jerked the blade out of the pine needles, he shoved hard with his other hand and pushed the raccoon alongside Tater. Instantly the animal gripped the limb and held on. Tater didn't care that it was there; he was too concerned about getting his breath.

Hastily Morgan maneuvered the oar upright in the water in order to get it into a better position for diving. He had to jam the blade between the two branches and pry them apart in order to remove the tangled line. He inhaled a long lungful of air and dived. With one hand, he felt his way down the nylon; with the other, he gripped the oar tip. He had very little room in which to work. If there had been any space between the branches, he would have been able to free the line easily. And deciding exactly which place was the best to get the leverage he needed to force the branches apart caused yet another delay. Still uncertain about the position, Morgan ran out of breath.

He surfaced as another wave swept over Tater and forced him underwater. Again Morgan grabbed the dog's head and pulled him back above the surface. But there was no more time to wait. Morgan gulped in another breath and dived.

Frantically he forced the strong ash oar into the small space allowed him. Above him he felt Tater moving and shifting his weight as he struggled for every life-saving breath. It was an incredibly tight fit. Morgan shoved the blade between the limb and trunk with every ounce of his strength. As it went into place, he felt the smaller limb move slightly under his hand. He surfaced.

"It's going to work!" But Tater was gasping for his breath; his head was thrown back, and his eyes rolled in terror. Morgan levered the oar backward violently. Suddenly the handle snapped and broke with a crack. At the same moment Tater lunged forward and shoved Morgan underwater unexpectedly.

The dog was free! Morgan thrashed to the surface, pushing Tater with him, and he shoved the dog into the maze of branches. Seconds later Tater was beside the raccoon. He hooked his front legs around the same limb and finally he was able to rest. Morgan swam up between them, clutched the pine needles, and held himself in place. Tater turned and pushed his nose into Morgan's neck.

"That was a close one!" he gasped weakly, as he leaned back against the branch. On one side, Morgan's head rested against Tater; on the other, his cheek brushed against the raccoon. They all held on for their lives.

Occasionally Morgan, afraid they might give up in exhaustion, roused himself to speak to the animals. The risk of either losing a grip on the limb and being swept away or slipping beneath the surface in sleep or unconsciousness was always present. There were times when he had to reach out and steady them as holding on was more difficult for the animals than for him. And they grew more tired with every passing minute.

Much later Morgan looked up. The raccoon had moved slightly and was looking around with its bright, dark eyes. The weary little animal seemed to have come back to life. Morgan frowned. Now he heard Tater breathing beside him. It was true the dog was only a few inches away from him, but until then he had been unable to hear a thing other than the screaming wind. Now the raccoon pointed his black nose at the sky. Morgan blinked.

Beyond a doubt the wind was going down. Not much, but it was slackening off, and the raccoon had sensed it first. Morgan didn't know how much

time had elapsed since the eye of the hurricane had gone over them, but the entire storm must have passed by. Now Tater was glancing from side to side; he was becoming interested in the world too.

Morgan readjusted his feet. All three of them were chest-deep in water and half supported on the submerged part of the tree that earlier had trapped Tater. Slowly Morgan began to feel his way farther up the branch and out of the water. He stretched upward knee-deep in the waves, and he peered around the fallen trees. Then he inched out of the water even more, and he stood staring at the horizon.

"The wind really has gone down," he croaked in amazement. He could stand up against it now and judged that it couldn't be blowing more than forty or fifty miles an hour. The worst definitely was over! The clouds were much higher in altitude, and there was no blackness to them. The storm was losing its grip. In this much wind the planes could fly. They would probably have to come from inland, but they should come right away.

Morgan closed his eyes. Until that moment he had succeeded in pushing thoughts of Mother to the back of his mind. Caught out in the middle of the marsh, he had been in no position to consider her safety. He moved restlessly. He knew very well the hurricane's winds probably had never reached over ninety miles an hour. And since some storms struck at well over two hundred miles an hour, this one had been a baby. There probably had been considerable damage, because it had arrived at the same time as high tide. The first floor of their house was liable to have been flooded. Morgan swallowed painfully. Everything would be ruined! Mother would not have been able to carry everything upstairs by herself.

But at least he didn't have to worry about Mother's safety. Even though he was missing, she would have been evacuated to high land. Still, he doubted if she would have gone to Grandmother's house in Varnville as long as he was still out in the marsh. She was probably sick with worry and fear but she at least would be safe and sound. The hurricane shelter they had built seven years ago in the basement of the high school could weather anything. And by now Father would have raced home from Charleston. Morgan knew he would be boiling over with impatience to come out on the marsh to look for him.

Morgan sighed. Relief was finally within sight! Oh to be safe and on high land, to be warm and filled with food, and to be dry!

He jerked himself out of his reverie, suddenly realizing that if a plane should fly over he needed some sort of signal to attract attention. Morgan touched the Very pistol in his belt and the two flares in his pocket to make certain they were safely in place. But he was not at all certain they would fire. They were supposed to be waterproof, but they had received some rough treatment.

Morgan looked across at the boat by the big pine. It was a wreck, but as the glistening fiberglass hull lurched and bobbed in the water upside down, the red bottom paint showed brilliantly. If he could push the boat away from the tree and get it out in sight, he could use it as a signal.

He turned his face into the wind again. It really had stopped blowing considerably, and the waves were not nearly as high. Then he saw the slicker he had left behind earlier, caught on a branch beside the boat. If he took the longer half of the broken oar, he could tie the pants to the end of it and make a signal flag.

Morgan was impatient to get over to the boat,

but he had to take the two animals along with him. He picked up the end of Tater's leash and pulled the dog off his perch. Then he turned to the raccoon, which stared at him quietly.

"You're coming, too," he said gently, and he shoved the little animal away from the limb. Within moments all three of them were making their way downwind, paddling and pushing debris aside as they went.

When they finally arrived at the boat, Morgan stared at it grimly. He couldn't possibly move it. The hole in the stern was immense! If he shifted it at all, the boat would sink like a rock. The only thing it was good for was to climb on and get out of the water. Morgan boosted Tater onto the flat bottom. Once on his feet the dog wagged his tail furiously and began to jump up and down happily. Next Morgan turned to the raccoon, which pawed at his arm. He lifted it up beside Tater onto the boat's bottom, and for a moment the two animals touched noses briefly before quietly settling down together. Morgan grinned. They seemed to have become fast friends!

But he had work to do! Morgan splashed over to his slicker and tied the shoulder straps securely to the end of the oar. The moment he held it upright in the wind, the pants streaked out in a blaze of bright yellow. Perfect! Now he had to find a spot to put his signal flag so that it could be seen from a plane.

The obvious place was to lay it along the pine's first lower limb and on the very end. It was out of the water, and the flag could wave away from the tree. In that position it could be seen easily from overhead. The problem was getting it out there. Morgan chewed at his lip. He would have to climb up to the branch, scramble out through the greenery, and lash it into place.

He pulled himself on top of the overturned boat with the animals. Instantly Tater was beside him dancing with enthusiasm, and he nearly pushed Morgan back into the water. His bouncing about made the boat lurch up and down precariously. Suddenly the raccoon slithered across the slick paint and landed in Morgan's lap. He laughed, helped the raccoon back to its feet, and then he stood up. He tossed his makeshift flag up into the tree, reached his hand over his head, and began to work his way upward into the branches.

"It won't be long now," he said cheerfully.

"We'll all—" Morgan sucked in his breath. At the same time he felt the hair on the back of his neck stand straight out. Just when he had begun to believe everything was going to be all right, the terror was back all over again.

A swamp rattler was dangling about a foot away from his face! Apparently when he had thrown the slicker flag into the tree, he had dislodged the deadly snake from its refuge. Now it had partially dropped off the limb and was holding itself in place with two loops of its body around the tree. Its tail sizzled with rattles, and as it swung in the wind, he saw its flat, wicked head and flicking, forked tongue. Morgan dared not move the slightest bit. If the snake was disturbed any more and it struck from where it was hanging, it would hit him right in the face.

Morgan swallowed. He suddenly realized the rattler was not as interested in him, locked in place like a statue, as it was in the slicker. The yellow rubber snapped and flapped noisily in the wind beside Morgan's head, and it was what the snake was eyeing nervously.

Carefully, inch by inch, Morgan lowered his arm. Slowly, bit by bit, he pulled the Very pistol out of his belt and then a flare from his pocket. Morgan told himself to hurry, yet he dared not risk attracting attention. Steadily and quietly Morgan turned the lever on the short, fat gun and broke open the barrel; he slipped the metal-cased, bronze shell inside. He could feel the perspiration dribbling down his cheek, but he kept his eyes riveted on the hissing, rattling snake that weaved back and forth directly in front of him. Slowly Morgan pulled up the barrel; it snapped into place with a click. The gun was loaded. Now he had to cock it.

But the pistol was stiff and heavy, and as Morgan pulled back the oversized hammer, his hand slipped; the gun moved sharply to one side. He gasped as the snake suddenly turned in the air. Now it had forgotten the annoying flapping flag, and it came straight for the gun in Morgan's hand! It rattled more furiously than ever, arching and raising its body as it dangled by its tail. Its head suddenly drew back. It was going to strike!

Morgan jerked up the gun and tried to pull the trigger. But he had forgotten how difficult it was to work. And now his frantic thrust upward put the barrel of the short gun within inches of the snake. The rattler darted at the metal, and at the same instant Morgan pulled the trigger with two fingers, and the flare gun went off.

The snake dropped off the limb and fell over Morgan's still-outstretched hands; then it slithered down his arm and across his life jacket. He lunged backward away from it and jerked the snake away from his chest. Then he stopped. Morgan stared at the horrible thing in his hand. The head of the snake had been shot off as neatly as if it had been guillotined. The next second an explosion boomed.

Arching above the tree was a high, smoking path, and farther aloft was the exploding, fiery blaze of a parachute flare.

Morgan fell back against the tree trunk in exhaustion, and he watched the red flare burn brightly and drift off to the east. Then he heard a faint sound above his head. Tater began to bark furiously, excitedly, with his muzzle raised to the sky. Morgan looked up.

Overhead, shining white with a brilliant slash of red stripes across its nose, was one of the large Coast Guard search seaplanes banking toward the burning signal flare.

"Oh!" Morgan gasped, and then he began to smile rapturously. Now that was sharpshooting!

In one shot he had not only killed a rattler, he had signaled salvation! Quickly he snatched up his makeshift flag and began to wave it wildly. And as if he knew rescue was at hand, Tater barked more loudly than ever.

"They see us! Oh, they see us!" Morgan shouted.

In only a few more minutes the plane landed, and the crew began to launch a rubber life raft. Then Morgan sucked in his breath; he could hardly believe his eyes. Father was with them!

Suddenly Morgan's thoughts flashed back to grim reality and to the fact that he had lost everything. But as the men paddled closer to the hammock and he was able to see Father clearly, Morgan knew everything was all right. The lost boat, the traps, the motor, nothing mattered at all. He should have realized it all along. Father was just bursting with happiness that they were alive.

Morgan kneeled on the overturned boat. Tater pushed his nose against his hand; the raccoon touched his arm with one small paw. In a few more minutes they would all three be going home.

Born in Nebraska and educated in California, Marian Rumsey is a travel enthusiast. She has lived aboard sailboats with her husband and two children for many years, and they have gone some 70,000 miles at sea. They also have traveled by land in a camper-truck. Between these two modes of transportation, they move about twelve months a year and cannot call any one city or state their home.

The author has written many articles about the family cruises and is well known in boating and yachting circles. She also writes general travel articles in addition to her children's books.